GET BACK

By #Clintington

Get Back

#Clintington

Visit:

clintington.com

There are always a number of people to thank. I have to thank my mother and sister. Mom for always reading my work when I ask her to and for loving it, even when it is a first draft bucket of shit. My sister, the woman my son calls "Aunt Bethy." She is my biggest critic, honest editor and highest supporter. Without these women in my life, some of these characters could never exist—quite literally. Last but not least is fellow author Nat Russo. If I had not stumbled upon him over the twitter-verse, I might never have completed this work. His expertise, documented journey as a writer, and courteous mentoring helped make this possible. You can follow him on twitter @NatRusso. If you're an aspiring writer with a twitter account and you're not following him; your loss. I should probably give my ex-wives a mention for inspiration…fuck that.

GET BACK

By #Clintington

December, 1996

That scrawny looking guy that looks out of place amongst all of these people having a good time. That's me. Not the one that lost his map to math lab and took a wrong turn, *he is wearing a sweet orange vest though over that nice collared long-sleeve black shirt. Go B's!* The other guy standing next to him with the beer in his hand; the guy with the glasses and the short ratty hair, that's me. I'm the host of this god awful festival if you can believe that. Look at all of those debauched little fools dancing around like its Mardi Gras. Well, at least I get to make sure the music is good at my own party. Once "Free Bird" hits the ears I know that it is time to jet. You won't hear that shit kick'n' piss tonight. Look at all those assholes and elbows banging together to some alternative tune that half of these people don't understand the words to or recognize. They have no concept of who the artist is, the name of the song, or why the poet wrote it. All they know is that it has a good beat to slam into each other with in unison so that no one falls over and gets trampled. I enjoy this kind of music for different reasons. Right now I just want to listen to the words and try to understand why this song is speaking to me in this moment. I don't know why he titled it after an anti-manic drug. Maybe it was because that is how he felt after taking it. Maybe that is how he thought he might feel if he took it, who knows? "... *happy...lonely...day...daze....*" Every time I hear it, I try to see myself doing and being those things that he describes. I never can relate it to mood altering medications, though since I've never taken them. Besides, I think an upper would be more appropriate. I might act like these guys and enjoy myself.

I used to have fun at these things, but lately I don't have

that much to cheer about. Now, before I continue, I'm writing this so you get a perspective of what it's like to be an average guy digging through a trough. I've hit some peaks, but as I write this, I tend to be in what I am hoping is a small gutter with low flow.

That girl's alone. I should go talk to her. I hate this part. This is the shit that I have never been good at. She's alone and waiting and I'm bumbling around with my hand in my pocket trying to think of something clever to say.

Oh, man. Asshole spilt beer all over me!

I didn't need that. It's one thing to be witless and dry, the wetness adds an anxious bonus. Now, before I take this plunge, I should probably give you a little back-story so that you get to know me before I make a total and complete jackass of myself while trying to woo this innocent girl with my evil man powers.

Four months ago my life changed...

September, 1996

I woke up to an empty bed and my unhappy girlfr—ex-girlfriend—was packing the remaining portion of her stuff. What the hell, right? Well, I kind of saw it coming, but no one —I'm talking no one—wants to go through what those days offer. So I got up and watched her finish packing. Yes, it was stressful and I did take my glasses off and rub my temples. You'll find that I do that a lot when I am trying to think of something clever to say.

She just kept packing that damn box and didn't act like I was even there. The packing kept getting louder and louder with each object that hit the bottom of that box.

Thump! Thump! THUMP! THUMP!

"Don't go. Please, I know how hard it is to live with me."

That's about as clever as it gets when I am stalling—pathetic, but honest.

She just kept packing that goddamn box as if I had not said anything at all.

THUMP! THUMP!

"Just...Can we talk some more?"

THUMP! THUMP!

"I know we hashed the hell out of this but...."

THUMP! THUMP!

"COULD YOU STOP PACKING FOR A SECOND AND LISTEN TO ME?!"

THUMP, went one more item as she crossed her arms and glared at me. I may have come on a little strong with that last request, but I got the result. It was probably the first time I had her full attention in the last six months.

"Thank you."

I had to stop and think for a second before I lit the fuse.

"Now I refuse to believe that this entire time that we've been together you weren't happy. How can you be with someone seven years and not tell that that you're unhappy?"

Question of fucking Questions if you ask me.

"We had fun." *PRESENT TENSE, PRESENT TENSE!* "We *have* fun." I stumbled over that one.

"I love Thursday mornings."

On Thursdays, we alternated making breakfast in bed for each other. We hadn't missed a Thursday in the seven years we lived together.

"You're a great cook."

Lie.

"That's our catch up day. I love breakfast. I . . . I love you."

Stalling again.

"Don't you see that? Now, I know that I am miserable, but I have always loved you. You're the only one I've been with since high school. If that ain't love, I don't know what is."

You can't see her face right now, but she is mentally slitting my throat; bad time for a joke.

"Seven years. Do you really believe we've been wasting our time? We can work it out."

When she stood up and picked up that box, my heart crushed my balls.

"You seem content. But, if you ever had a feeling at all that we weren't doomed from the beginning, you'll empty that box and talk to me. But if you leave, that means you never *really* loved me. It was just words every time you said it." *Heartless manipulation, I know, but she was leaving with the last box.*

There was a blissful moment there when I looked up into her eyes and I thought for a split second that I had her, but her mind was made up. When she slammed the door behind her, it was a slap to the face. I got up and had to say something.

"Seven fucking years!" I shouted at her. "What a cliché!"

It's unfortunate that I *am* one of those "has-to-have-the-last-word" kind of guys. Even though she didn't say anything the whole time, that door slam was louder than any of those expletives I yelled at her. So I tried to slam the door louder than her a couple of times, but it just never seemed to get as loud as hers no matter how much force I put into it.

I don't remember a lot of the details that day, except when I broke the news to my "friend(s)". You have to tell someone. They'll find out eventually and it's just better to get it off your chest. It was after practice, and I had a *shitty* practice. Everyone noticed. My best friend Billy sat down next to me after practice when we were taking our cleats and shinguards off. I only had what happened with Randy on my mind, as you can imagine.

"Whew, I am one sweaty bastard," he said. "I think that was all right for me any way. You okay?"

No, my girlfriend left me. How are you?

I really said, "Randy left me."

I thought that he was going to throw up. I guess that's how best friends react.

"Fuck you, serious?" he asked.

I just gave him a look and he understood *how* serious I was.

"Fuck, sorry man. What happened?"

I was surprised by all the expletives. He doesn't curse a lot—especially with the "for unlawful carnal knowledge" word. I didn't know that I had it in me to make him swear so much.

I couldn't answer his question. I needed more time to think about it, but I didn't particularly want to be alone, either.

"Let's go to Emery's and we'll talk about it. I don't want to do it here."

Just a side note, Emery's is my favorite sports bar. Wonderful food, any beer you want, and—it's locally owned so there are no corporate douche bags worried about sales and expanding. *Fucking Cheers man.*

Anyways, as I invited Billy to the bar, I didn't notice the tall drinks of water standing behind me; Davy and Brock. I would call them friends, but with friends like these—well, I guess all best friends give each other shit, that's why they're your *best* friends. Musketeer wise, Davy is to Aramis as Brock is to Porthos as Billy is to Athos. Yeah, I'm fucking d'Artagnan. I'm telling the story, I'm d'Artagnan.

So, not noticing them, they heard "Emery's" and their ears perked up.

"Emery's? I'm down," said Brock.

Before I could say anything, Billy blabbed, "Randy left him."

"Fuck off man. Serious?" asked Davy.

I couldn't describe the look I threw Billy. I don't think he felt comfortable with his back facing me the rest of that evening.

"Well, let's go get some pizza bombs," suggested Brock.

"And beer," Davy added as he looked at me and shook his head. "Shit man."

We made it across the street and started talking after we sat and ordered our food. I was definitely ready for sympathy night, but Brock and Davy weren't selling.

"She basically told me she never *really* loved me," I continued. "I know I'm a fucking asshole, but come on, I made some sacrifices for her."

That was the point at which I hoped the conversation would lead to my "friends" reminding me of *all* the sacrifices I did indeed actually make, but they weren't going to tug on that line.

"Like what," asked Brock.

I wanted to knock the smug bastard off the back of his bar stool.

"Like staying here instead of trying out," I quickly reminded him. "I went to school because she wanted me to. I wanted to go try out for the *Foxes*…didn't happen…I stayed here for her."

"You were *really* going to try out?" asked Davy, raised eyebrow in tow.

What the fuck?

"YES…as sure as you're sitting there."

I couldn't let him think that I wouldn't.

"So go try out now man, you're free," said a positive (and appreciated) Billy.

"Next year man. I missed this year. Next year."

Brock shook his head wearing a pompous smile, "I

think that's your problem right there."

"What?" I asked.

"You're always putting shit off. There's no decision making, just excuses."

"Nice Brock," said Billy.

At the same time I said, "What the fuck man?"

All Brock could muster at that point was, "Hey, I'm just saying."

My steam whistle was getting ready to go off.

"Do you have to say it now? Dickhead! My girlfriend just left me after seven fucking years. The only woman I've ever been with."

All three of them sipped their beer and ate their pizza. I lost my appetite. It was very uncomfortable. Davy broke the silence.

"Brock makes a good point though."

"Don't encourage him," said Billy.

Davy replied, "No, hear me out."

He looked at me and smiled, I didn't want to hear what he had to say, but I knew I was going to.

Davy continued, "When *did* you finally declare a major?"

Low blow.

Everyone knew I didn't want to be in school, so how the hell was I supposed to pick a major. I replied honestly.

"When I had to."

I wanted to call *him* a dickhead, but I don't think he would have heard me.

"How many times did you switch majors?"

The fucking questions! I just wanted them to eat and leave.

"Five times."

I couldn't look at them. I just looked up at one of the televisions and drank my beer. I didn't care what was on; it could've been "Beverly Hills 90210" for all I cared. I wasn't going to look at those assholes.

I could feel their eyes on me for a split second. I know those two bastards shared a smug glance with each other.

Discomfort.

Damn silence.

"What kind of friends would we be if we didn't point out the obvious," asked Davy.

At least the douche bag broke the awful silence.

"The kind that do it later," said Billy.

I could have kissed him. He took the words right out of my mouth.

He continued, "Like not the day that someone's been fucked over. I know he's an asshole—hell he does."

"I do," I said.

Please continue sir.

"It doesn't mean he needs to hear this shit right now from you assholes."

They ARE assholes! I don't know why I hang out with those two.

"Well he needs to hear this," Brock spouted off.

"I'm sitting right here," I wanted to hit him. No one likes it when they're being talked about like they're not there.

"You need to hear this," agreed Davy.

Motherfucker! I want to kick his ass too.

"You guys are out of line," said Billy.

Speechless for too long, I got sick of the silence. I did what every guy I know does when he is having a conversation that is going nowhere and he no longer wants to have it.

"I gotta take a piss."

And I did.

I didn't see it, but I imagine Billy shook his head like he always does when he's disgusted beyond words.

I don't think I'd do that to them if they were in this circumstance. I don't think they know better....but sometimes, friends feel that being self-righteous is the only way to be a *true* friend. That's Brock and Davy.

So the day after my friends reminded me of what an asshole *I* was, we had a game. The game was not one to be remembered, but what I do recall was very interesting—I "shared a moment" with someone at that game.

Okay, that sounds weird, I know, but I'm banking on it's not what you think. I'm not the kind of guy to get sappy and write about what a wonderful, kooky experience I had and how it changed my life for the better. As much as it changed me, I don't have a gift of visions where I go from town-to-town helping people change their futures. *Like Kane from "Kung fu"...that would be badass*—but...no, not that kind of "moment." I don't write those stories. I write what I know and I know that it was a perception, but it was a little more selfish than the average, uh, "gift." That's probably why I don't write those kinds of stories. Yet again, we are aware that I'm an asshole; well established.

I remember the whistle clear as day as the ref called a foul on Billy for tackling from behind. The next thing I know me, Davy, Billy and Brock are setting up the "wall". Davy was on my left facing the ball. Billy was on my right facing the ball. Brock was next to Davy with his back to the ball as he looked to our keeper for directions.

I always get jazzed up when I'm standing in the wall. It is one of the few experiences in life that can be generally physically painful, but emotionally rewarding at the same time. It was different that day, my mind wasn't in the game.

I remember looking into the stands for any sign of Randy.

I also felt that was a *great* moment to share my pain and frustration aside to Billy. I'm not sure why, but when you feel shitty, you just want to talk about it...a lot. To anyone that will listen.

"I can't believe it was all a sham. I thought she loved me."

Billy humored me.

"She fooled all of us," he said, a little distracted.

Yeah, my head was not in the game.

"Man, seven years. All on one girl," I said as I turned to Billy. "One fucking girl."

"Well," he replied lowly, "you have to admit, you haven't actually been beating them off with a stick my friend."

I jerked my head toward him and glared.

Startled by the abrupt and honest comment from Billy, I heard the ref blow the whistle and as I turned back to react, I remember seeing a white and black checkered sphere spinning toward me as blackness flashed.

Yes. Right in the forehead between my eyes.

It all happened in slow motion when I thought about it later. I remember being able to read the *Adidas* label on the ball right before it struck my head.

Billy told me I was out for over a minute.

The light faded in and I opened my eyes. I woke up to Billy's out-of-focus mug standing over me. He was smiling like he just got laid.

"Bright side—you saved a goal," he said.

Like I'm concerned about the score—we were getting our asses kicked. I sat up, moaned, wiped the drool/snot from my mouth and felt that red spot on my forehead. When I stood in the mirror later I could read *adidas*; that meant everyone else saw: **sabiba**.

"Bad news—I think you gotta concussion dude."

Billy helped me up and I don't remember walking off the field. I was thinking that it was going to be a late night talking to Billy because I knew that asshole wouldn't let me sleep if he thought I had a concussion.

I guess everyone clapped when I got up and walked off. Funny thing, the biggest cheer I ever got while playing was when I had to leave the game because of an injury (I didn't score a lot of goals). Billy helped me off with one arm over his shoulder and I made my way.

Now, I don't know why, but it was like the sun was a perfect spotlight on that girl I saw in the stands. She stood up from her seat and began walking down the stairs, all in slow motion of course.

I made it off the field as she was making her way down the stadium steps when our eyes met. She stopped and I felt my heart race. My head was heavy. Something was going to give. Billy lost his grip on me and I hit the ground, knees first. My head followed as it slammed into the track that enveloped the barrier of the field.

I remember what I saw when I was out again, but it was difficult to describe. I was in my apartment, it was dark, and there were a lot of people. I couldn't hear anything, but everyone looked like they were having a good time mingling, and some were jumping and dancing to the music I couldn't hear. I was floating through the crowd, not flying above them, just hovering through them. I was drawn to a light that was coming from an open door. Everyone else there didn't notice it like I did. I know because I checked. I felt invisible. I walked through the door. I saw the girl I noticed at the stadium as I passed through the doorway and the spotlight hit her at the end of my tunnel vision.

I wanted to find out who she was.

I know that I was "awake" at the game, but everything was fuzzy and I didn't start to remember anything until after I got home. Billy was there to make sure that I was okay. Good guy, but I remember being annoyed because I was tired and wanted to sleep. He wouldn't let me. Like I said, I had an awesome new forehead tattoo. He went and got an ice pack ready and told me to put it over my **sabiba**.

I was inebriated and I just started talking about whatever came to mind. Of course I talked about *her*.

"Did you see her Billy?"

"Who?"

"I'm not sure, some girl."

I felt so tired and wanted to doze off. Billy humored me; allowing me to babble on.

"She was so…so pretty. She…was sweet looking and gentle. I noticed her leaving as I fell. She had her hair up in a ponytail."

"I love the ponytail," he said.

"Me too," I replied. "It's so…so cute. She had this delicate little smile. Her hair bobbed up and down as she descended the steps."

I remember seeing her face in that moment.

"There was this holy glare about her as if she were the only one that stood out among one-hundred people. I wish I would've gotten her number."

"Okay," he said. "You got hit really hard."

I did.

It was a cold day; wet and cloudy. Robin woke up and didn't bother with a shower. She was excited and wanted to get a good seat at the stadium. She enjoyed acting like it'd be a full stadium. Denial was everything as a soccer fan in America.

She threw on some jeans and a white t-shirt on her way to the bathroom. She brushed her teeth and checked her thick brown eyebrows, tweezing them to ensure they were even. It was unnecessary as they were perfect upside-down soft "v" shapes that accentuated her green eyes. She finally put her gentle brown hair into a delicate ponytail and called that good for her morning grooming.

She was grabbing her jacket and gloves when she heard a knock at her door. Before she could answer, the person at the door helped herself in.

"Missy," Robin said with joy in her voice. "You made it. I didn't think you'd come, and you're early."

Missy, a little rough for wear, asks through a yawn as she delicately raised two small fingers to cover her gentle lips, "We're getting coffee later, right?"

"Yes, I'll get you coffee."

"Okay, let's go," said Missy, as they headed out the door.

* * *

In the stands it was a slow start for the home team and the visiting team appeared to be at the top of their play. Fifteen minutes in and the home team was down two nothing. Robin's voice was starting to grow horse, as she was one of the few fans shouting and singing. Missy decided to stand with her as they both belted out the school song:

Fight, Fight, Fight! We're the best in the west-So green are the rest-Gnash your teeth-Bare your claws-Drive with all your might-Fight! Fight! Fight!-You Decide our fate-Bring the victory home to us--Ohhhh Biiig Staaate.....!

"GO B's!" shouted Missy.

Missy, feeling tired and woozy, took a seat.

"GO B's!" shouted Robin.

"Rob, that was fun, but I'm sorry, I need to get some breakfast," said Missy. "I thought I could make it, but I totally forgot to eat before I came over."

"Oh," said Robin with disappointment in her tone. "Can we leave at halftime? It's almost over."

"Of course," said Missy. "That's what I meant, at half."

Robin sat next to Missy.

"They really are not playing that well today," said Robin. "So," changing the subject, "have a little too much fun last night?"

Missy, watched the game, refusing to make eye-contact with Robin who was now smiling and looking at her, "Maybe," she replied with a smile of her own.

"Too much drinking, or too much men?"

"Both," said Missy blushing, still refusing to look at Robin.

Robin looked back at the game.

"Okay, Switch! No! Right wing! Wide open," shouted Robin, standing now.

To Missy, "He was wide open, did you see that," sitting back down.

Missy humored her with a nod, concentrating not to doze off.

Robin continued coaching, "Get back! Right side, contain! Back, back! Foul! FOUL!"

The whistle was blown on the field as one of the home players took Robin's advice. The visiting team was issued a free kick.

Robin stood, shouting, "Wall, WALL!"

Missy was starting to look sick and gagged, while deep breathing. "Okay, I need to go," said Missy.

"Okay," Robin said, wrapping a blanket around her friend.

"You can finish the half, I'll meet you at the car."

Missy got up and started making her way down the stadium steps.

Robin stood and gathered her blanket as well.

Robin continued to watch the game, looking up in between steps down. Missy treated it like a race down the steps and was almost at the bottom. The whistle was blown for the awarded free kick. Robin paused from her descent. Just before the ball was kicked, Robin made eye contact with one of the home players in the wall for a split second. The player was blindsided by the ball in the face and shriveled to the ground like a puppet when the strings are released.

Robin gasped and whispered, "Oh my God," under her breath.

Robin continued her delayed descent as she watched players gather around the injury on the field. He appeared to be conscious. He was helped up and off the field by one of his teammates. She reached the bottom as the injured player and his teammate reached the sideline.

They made eye contact again. Robin gave a half smile to the dazed player.

He tumbled to the ground, hitting his head pretty hard, again.

Robin gasped deeper this time and covered her mouth with her hands, feeling as though it was her fault this time, "Oh no," under her breath. "That's gonna hurt for a while."

"What'd I miss," asked Missy as she noticed the second fall by the player to the ground.

"He got hit in the head with the ball."

"He's cute," said Missy, holding back another gag.

Robin smiled, attending to Missy, "Let's get you some eggs," putting an arm around her as they walked back to the car.

* * *

After class, Robin prepared for practice. She put on her gear and headed down to the field. At the field, she put on her cleats and led the team in stretches with the other captain. It was not too arduous; drills, and then a scrimmage. She laughed and caught up with her teammates during water brakes and afterward she took off her cleats and walked back to her dorm.

Another day, another practice.

With all of her gear in tow in a sports-bag that she carried over her right shoulder, Robin headed up the main dorm steps. She noticed two perfect looking girls at the top of the stairs heading past her. She always found them intimidating, and tried to keep her head down when she walked past. She continued up the steps past the beautiful girls, trying to keep her sports-bag from jutting out into the aisle and blocking their path. As they passed, Robin perceived an annoyed, judgment on her as they watched. Once she was clear of them, she heard them giggle as they walked out the door. She hoped they weren't laughing at her.

Robin carried on up the stairs. She entered her room and set her bag on the floor. She took a brief moment to lay on her bed, and looked up at the ceiling. Thoughts of that boy she saw get injured at yesterday's game started to float through her head.

Feeling a little lonely, she forced herself to pick up her backpack and attempt to start her homework. She pulled out a book and a pen and right before she started to read it-

Thump, thump, thump, at the door.

Startled and confused, Robin sets down her things and goes to her door. She swings the door inward and standing there in front of her is the injured guy at yesterday's game.

"Hi," she said.

"Hi, how are you?"

She giggles. He holds her in his arms, as she looks up at him.

She wore a big smile while she daydreamed and looked up at the ceiling from her bed. There was a pleasant and warm feeling at the top of her stomach.

* * *

An unfocused Robin walked from class-to-class the next day with a glazed over expression. As she exited one door of the building, she didn't notice the "cute guy" entering the opposite door of the same building in that moment.

Robin unconsciously pulled out her mittens from the front central pocket of her sweatshirt. They were mittens that her grandmother made her for Christmas. There was a red "R" sewn on her right mitten and a red "M" sewn on her left mitten. Robin turned the corner and noticed Missy in the middle of the Quad talking to the girls she passed on the steps yesterday.

Robin envied Missy's ability to talk to people, and make friends. It always came easy to her. *Well, at least I have Missy to introduce me to people,* Robin thought with a grin.

She took a deep breath and walked over to them.

Robin caught the end of their conversation.

"Friday at two," asked Missy. "Okay, I think I can be

there."

"Okay, it'll be so nice to see you there," said the taller of the young girls.

Robin felt invisible again as she gave a gentle tug on Missy's sleeve.

Startled a little, Missy turned and saw that it was Robin and was relieved.

"Oh, hi Rob," she said with a smile and a side hug, "Guys, this is my best friend, Robin."

Robin shook their hands.

"Hi, you're the soccer girl, right, you live at Owen" asked the shorter girl.

"Yes," Robin replied, feeling herself blush a little. "I have to lug that gear around all the time." She was a little surprised that they remembered her. "And you are?"

"Oh, I'm sorry," said the shorter blonde. "I'm Krystal and this is Sandra."

"We were just telling Missy about a party we're throwing on Friday. It starts at two," said Sandra.

"Yeah, I heard, I have a game so I doubt I can make that."

"Oh," said Krystal with disappointment on her face. "Well, it *starts* at two, maybe you could come after."

"And miss her studying….God forbid," said Missy with a giggle.

Robin felt the blush turn on again, as she gave a slight giggle.

"Well, we hope to see you soon, if you can't make that. It was nice to meet you," said Sandra as they both walked off.

"Thank you," said Robin. "Nice to meet you too."

"I'll see you Friday," said Missy as she waved goodbye.

"You didn't have to do that," said Robin.

"I'm sorry," said Missy. "You can come with me then.

We'll show up fashionably late after your game."

"Well, I *do* have to study…."

Robin realized how right Missy was.

Missy just smiled and looked at her.

"Shut up Missy."

Both of them giggled.

"You headed to class or do you have time for lunch," asked Missy.

"I just got out of class. Let's eat. You're buying."

So…pretty good week. I got a concussion, *those are always relaxing*; we lost our game—*handedly*; my head still hurts like a motherfucker; *not to mention the fact that I also have that pretty sweet looking red "**sabiba**" tattooed on my forehead —not by choice and oh yeah*; my now ex-girlfriend has left; *hence ex*. I am dealing with some serious shit here as I walk from class to class with Billy blabbing about how wonderful his façade that he refers to as a life is going. I am walking around like a zombie, and all I can think about is Randy. I want her back so bad. I don't care how she treats me. I just miss her.

"So when are we going to get shitfaced over this terrible mishap of yours?"

My friends, you'll find, have a tendency to say the right thing at the wrong time. I would love to get drunk, I just don't want to "plan it." It's one of those things that should just happen—sort of. My friends always need a reason to go get drunk; they have girlfriends. I'm jealous, but at the same time, I like the idea of being able to do what I want when I want to now. I haven't had that for a *long* time and I want to see if I can still do that. My friends however still have to say things like, "Matthew really needs me right now baby. His girl just left him." Code = "We're going out tonight. It will be late. Don't stay up and don't expect a call."

"I don't feel like alcohol would be the best thing for me right now."

You should see his face right now.

I don't think that I have ever turned him down for an opportunity to go drinking, unless Randy told me "No," which happened A LOT now that I think about it.

"I just need to clear my head and move on. I need to

get out of this town," I continued.

"We could go to"

"I'm not going to Vegas, *Trent* ("Swingers" reference)," I cut him off because I knew that he wanted to go *somewhere* in Nevada.

NOT what I need right now.

"Okay," he said. "I was going to say Jack Pot. Vegas is like a million miles away man. Come on, you need to get out of town, you said so yourself."

"I meant *permanently*. I just can't…" I had to stop.

I hate sharing these parts. I feel like such a baby.

I started getting "the hurt." You assholes that have lost someone know what I'm talking about. You try and hold back the pain and the crying and it just takes a siesta in your throat. You try and swallow to slow it down. I was able to strangle away the tears—for a while.

"She's just gone," I said.

He stood there—speechless. I held it together for a little while, but Billy knew that I was going to lose it in public and he was very uncomfortable.

"What am I doing here man?"

No response. His eyes opened a little wider. I DO have his attention.

"I have never liked it here. I stayed for her. I hate that she is not there when I go home. That's bad, but it's not the worst part."

I have a few tears now. His eyes are wide open now, as he starts to look around in discomfort.

"The worst is when you are in between awake and sleep and you reach over…" I'm losing it now, glasses off, waterfalls being wiped away—no snot yet though. "…and her warm body isn't there anymore. I used to love waking up next to her."

There's the snot.

"Man," he said. "I wish I knew what to say, but honestly I don't know."

I was really making him feel uncomfortable now. I could not control the amount of snot that decided to flow out of my nose. I felt like shit.

He can't decide whether to put his arm on my shoulder or not...

"I want to say that everything will be okay, but I just don't know. Nobody knows."

It's VERY obvious he is lost.

"Yeah, I feel like it is getting worse," I said while blowing my nose into my right elbow sleeve.

He looks like he wants to gag now, but he wants to be supportive. Good guy.

"I feel so depressed," I say as everything starts to flow out of my face, tears, snot, sweat—it was an open fire hydrant of human ooze. Billy finally put his arm around me at that point.

"Shhhhhhhh….."

He actually "shhhh'd" me.

"Things have to get better….time…ah fuck it man, just let it out."

He put both arms around me as I had my head across his shoulder. I moaned like a sick cow. I know that people were starting to gather around us now. You can feel the eyes all over your back.

Billy let go of me. I moaned louder after I caught my breath. I was piling it on a little because I knew how uncomfortable it made Billy feel—but I *did* feel like shit.

"Okay man, people are looking now," he said aside to me.

The next shameless thing I said and did was purely for the drama of the moment.

"I FUCKING LOVE HER MAN!"

"I know."

What else is he going to say, really?

I looked up and there were actually *way* more people than I thought and I felt rather foolish at that point.

"Shit," I cleared my throat, took my glasses off again, and wiped my eyes. "I need some coffee."

Billy looked up at the crowd and could not believe that everyone was still staring. I didn't like it much either, but he got really wigged out.

"Okay, you guys trying to do an Etch-a-Sketch," he shouted at the gathering. "Go on, he's okay, make your way to your classes please. Thanks for the concern."

The crowd slowly dispersed, not fast enough for Billy.

He raised his voice this time, "Thanks! He's fine!"

I got my shit together and started wiping my face down.

"Fuck class," I said. "Not in the mood. Philosophy is bullshit anyway."

"I have to go," he said. "O-chem is a bitch."

"I'll be fine. I've kept you from class too long already."

"I'll call you. We'll eat later."

"Yeah, see ya."

* * *

So, that night we ended up at *Emery's*, as usual, and we played chess while we were waiting for our food. For the record, even when my mind is not preoccupied with life's bullshit, Billy still kicks my ass at chess.

"I feel so pathetic lately, and the only thing I can think about is having more sex," I said as I moved some rook somewhere on that checkered piece of shit.

Billy quickly moves his knight right after I let go of my rook, "Me too, except for the *pathetic* part."

"Why don't you guys just do it," I ask him as I move a

piece on the board.

"She wants to wait."

"I don't get that. What if you're terrible at fucking?"

Now, I know that I'm being crass, but I have just had my heart broken. I also understand that I am on borrowed time with that excuse. I'm *really* horny right now and not thinking straight. That happens to me more often than I like.

"Hey, I know you're upset with your current status, but you don't need to drag me down into your despair. *I'm* here for *you*."

I'm not taking any shit from him right now.

"Yeah, then have sex. You can you know."

Why am I doing this? Oh yeah, my girlfriend left me and this is my "social life" right now. It's this or sleep.

"*I* want to wait too," he says as he moves another piece on the board. "Check."

"Liar!"

I moved my king to safety in case you assholes were worried about the chess match.

"*She* wants you to wait, that's why you're waiting."

It's true. As cool as Ashley is—and she's freaking awesome—she's a bit uptight in the sex before marriage department.

Billy moves another piece on the board.

"Check," he said, ignoring me.

He passive-aggressively tried to re-direct me with a chess move, but I can lose at chess and bitch at the same time.

"You two are victims of your own choosing. If you want to fuck, fuck; don't tell me you want to wait. We both know you're not a virgin."

"Check mate," he said as he moved his queen in for the kill.

I triple checked the board. He boned me in record time I think.

"We need to finish any way," he said. "Ashley's here."

Okay, I'm not going to lie to you guys. I have a crush on Ashley. It's innocent and she's the best, even with the sex thing. She's one of the coolest people I know. I think sometimes Billy gets nervous that he's going to lose his best friend status with me and Ashley will take it over. He should be. Now that I think about it, he's the uptight one. The sex thing *was* probably his idea. *That makes her even cooler!*

He looked behind me like he was waving her over.

I turned and looked and there she was. I got out of my booth and headed toward her. It'd been a while since I'd seen that feisty little read head. With our school schedules and Randy, I didn't have much time to hang with her.

Hopefully that will change.

"Matty boy," she said with a smile.

I gave her a big hug and picked her up off the ground.

"How you doing little sis?"

"Who cares, how are you?"

There was a little too much concern in that last question.

He told her.

I turned and gave Billy a death glare, "I wanted to tell her," I said.

He gave an uncomfortable giggle back, "Sorry man, we talk."

"I asked you to let me tell her," I said as Ashley and I made it back to the booth.

"He has a hard time keeping things from me," she said as she took her jacket off and hung it on a hook by the booth. "Can you blame him?"

"A little," I replied as she sat down. "You still wear the skirts, right?"

Ashley giggled, "Now be nice."

"You know I can't keep secrets, especially from her,"

Billy said.

"You guys aren't even married yet," I said. "I'll never be able to tell you anything after that happens. I'll have to hang out with Ashley exclusively."

"Hey," said Billy. "She can't keep things from me either."

"Oh yes she can."

Billy looked at her for clarity.

"Sorry babe," she said. "I *can* keep a secret."

"How so," he asked.

"Did you know that Randy and I were having problems for a while," I asked him.

"Well, no."

"I did," said Ashley as she raised her hand.

"What, you talked to her about it?"

"Yes," I said. "And I asked her not to tell *anyone* about it."

"And I didn't," said Ashley.

"You told Davy and Brock right after I told you," I said. "I don't think my grandma would've cracked that fast."

Ashley giggled.

"I don't like secrets," is all he could say.

"Oh, we know," I replied.

The server walked up at that point to take Ashley's order. Pulled pork sandwich with fries.

Billy or I could've ordered that for her. We should've.

Ashley's the kind of friend you keep for life. She keeps you at ease, she's a great listener, she's funnier than you could ever be, but she'll put you in your place when your head gets too big, and she also knows when you need to hear what you need to hear.

Billy's a good listener too. He has to be. When all of us hang out, Ashley and I do most of the talking and laughing. I kind of feel bad for him, a little. Then I remember he's chosen not to have sex with this cool chick and I don't feel bad at all. Maybe he's a bad lay and doing her a favor, who knows?

I'd bang her. I mean, I WON'T bang her, but I WOULD bang her if I was Billy.

I couldn't. She's too much a friend. I know I'm not a good lay....wouldn't put her through that. I value our friendship.

Anyways...Billy isn't much of an NFL fan. He likes English Premiere League soccer. I do too, but I have more access to the NFL. Ashley is definitely my drinking-beer-watching-football-on-Sundays buddy. Billy's present during all of this, but he doesn't get it like we do while bonding. So, when I say I have a "crush" it's a "bro crush" even if she is a chick; she's one of my best "bros."

Also, Ashley's a better story teller, she has a better sense of humor, and she's got an outgoing personality.

They actually make sense. Billy's a nice quiet intellectual that is into science, literature, and soccer.

"So....one of the coolest things happened to me today."

She starts every story off like that. They're hit and miss, but she believes it.

"I got into the elevator at the BA building and this massive wall of a man got in next to me and pushed the button. I just got out of my history class and the professor had asked us to think about what we wanted to be when we grow up. She threw out some stats--I can't remember the numbers--about how the majority of people that graduate college do not end up in the profession that they studied in school....anyways, I got to thinking about that and you guys know I don't like silences so as we started up the floors for a few seconds I broke it by engaging with The Wall next to me-"

See what she did there? Already that guy is now "The Wall," that's storytelling...

The server brought her food. She went right on telling

her story as she prepared to eat her meal.

"-'I got asked what I wanted to be when I grow up today.' Silence. He just raised an eyebrow and looked in my general direction without saying anything. Well I couldn't let that go, so I asked him, 'What do you want to be when you grow up,' she said as she took a bite out of her sandwich.

"He gave me that same pompous eyebrow raise, looked down at me again and said, 'A football player,' she said with a bite of sandwich in her mouth.

We were used to the full mouth talking.

She continued.

"The elevator opened on his floor and he walked off. I said, 'Well that's a lofty dream,' shouting it behind him as he walked off. I didn't think much of it, other than I thought he was an 8 year old that was never told, 'Not gonna happen buddy,' until I found out who he was," she turned her head to the left looking at the wall.

We both looked up at the same picture on the wall of the current Quarterback in uniform with the ball cocked over his right shoulder.

Billy and I both looked back at her, "Brian Twig!"

Twig, at the time, was the only reason our school was relevant on the national stage. He had NFL scouts coming to games since he got the start last year as a sophomore and there were major expectations for him and the team this year. Long story short, he was going to be a football player in the NFL.

We all started laughing.

All I could think to giggle was, "That's awesome."

We bullshitted through the rest of her meal and eventually Billy got up to use the restroom and pay the bill.

"Seriously though, how are you?"

Everyone knew I wasn't great, especially Ashley. It was hard for me because for the last three years, all four of us did things together. Ashley and Randy seemed pretty close. I felt like I was letting my friends down by not making it work with Randy…*I don't know how to tell her that.*

So I said what every guy would say.

"I'm okay," my voice squeaked that out a little.

Ashley just gave me the *"Really?"* eyes.

"What do you want me to say? I am okay; I'm not great. I wish I could get better a little faster; doing this stuff with you guys helps."

"Was that so hard, asshole?"

I smiled.

"Yes," I said quietly under my breath.

"Billy's not here and I'm not gonna tell him you said that."

"I appreciate that, wouldn't care if you did."

"You don't have to worry about Randy, she left us too. All you have to do is call and we can hang out and talk."

"Thank you."

Billy walked up on us after that and stood waiting for Ashley to join him.

"So," she continued as she stood and gathered her jacket, "are we going to Dudley's Sunday?"

"Same bat-time…"

"I'll see you at practice tomorrow," said Billy.

* * *

I stayed in bed for the next two days.

I called coach to let him know that I wasn't going to be at practice. School could wait too. I wasn't sick. I didn't want to do anything except feel sorry for myself. There is self-loathing, crying, sweat, snot, tears—it all sounds bad, but there is worse. *The Unknown.* The entire time that you are lying there waiting and thinking, you are only concerned about where you go from here and what will happen next. Oddly, nothing happens when you lie in your bed all day, but that is beside the point and that anticipation is why you are lying there in the first place. You are too afraid to take a chance on doing *anything* that might make you feel even worse. So you do nothing, which makes you feel worse because all you have to do there is think about how bad you feel and how much worse it is going to get.

It's a *wonderful* state of mind to be in.

So, my "friends" with impeccable timing decided to stop in and save the day. Actually, it wasn't really like that. They were just stopping by to see if I remembered that we had made plans a while ago to see the lady *B*'s play *We State*. I was at my apartment, down in my room on my bed. They were outside at the front door and I could hear everything that they said. It seemed like my depression had given me "Spidy Sense" hearing. Honestly, you just listen better when you're depressed because you're *always* hoping that someone might say that *one thing* that will lift you up and get you off your growing ass. So I sat there—content—listening.

Thump! Thump! Thump!

"Hey Matt! Come on baby."

It was Billy. He continued with the annoying knocking.

Thump! Thump! Thump!

I just sat there, bundled up in my blanket with my arms crossed. I was pouting as my eyes started to water.

I was touched. At the time, I had forgotten that we had made plans. I thought that I *actually* had friends who cared about me…then they started talking.

"Come on Matt," Billy continued. "We missed you at practice…and school. It's been a couple days now. We want you to come to the game with us. Remember?"

"Dude," it sounded like Brock. "We're gonna miss kickoff."

Yep, Brock.

"I don't care!"

That's why Billy's my best friend.

"Come on Matt," he said as he continued knocking.

Thump! Thump! Thump!

"It'll be great to get your mind off things."

Billy was right. I could use the fresh air and the sun.

"He doesn't want to go," that was most likely Davy. "Let's just go. We can check on him after the game."

Billy ignored them and continued knocking.

Thump! Thump! Thump!

"Come on Matty. We're going to miss kickoff."

It started to sound like Billy was losing faith. I needed to get off my ass. I stood up, wiped the tears off my face, and went to my front door.

"Let's go," said Brock.

"I'm not leaving until he gets up," said Billy.

Honestly, I was just about to open the door, but I was so touched that Billy was standing up for me that I lost it again on the other side of the door. I tried to be quiet and hold it in which made it hurt even worse; another "throat pain siesta."

"We could miss the entire game," yet again, Davy was annoyed with my drama.

"Do you even care how he's doing," said Billy.

I wanted to cry again, but I got it together.

"The guy missed practice. Have you ever known him to do that?"

Silence.

"I've never known him to miss practice. Last year he showed up with a 102 fever and snot running down his nose. Coach had to take him to the ER."

It's true. I had a bronchial infection. I didn't think anyone knew, except coach.

"This is the guy who made it to practice with a bronchial infection."

See.

"Don't you care," he shouted at them.

I wasn't able to see Davy and Brock's expressions, but I don't think that Billy's words made any type of lasting impression.

"Fuck you guys," he said. "Just go. I'm not leaving without talking to him first."

I do love Billy.

I needed that pick-me-up, so I flipped the latch and opened the door.

The looks on Davy's and Brock's faces made me feel a lot better; in a devious way. To see their faces after knowing that they knew I heard what they had said was like catching your dieting girlfriend with a carton of Haagen-Dazs in the corner of her room with the small fridge hidden under a pile of dirty clothes. You're disappointed, but you gotta respect the planning and scheming of it all and at the end of the day, you just want to say, "Eat some fucking ice cream."

"Hey Matt, what's up," said Brock.

"Matt," said a startled Davy. "How are you? Did you just wake up?"

What a pair of assholes. They belong together. I'm wearing a ratty ass t-shirt and boxers, I have *extreme* bed hair, and morning eye boogers. I didn't say anything. I just looked at Davy until he looked away. After an uncomfortable silence, I finally spoke.

"Just—go to the game. Billy and I will catch up."

Billy stepped into my apartment.

I took a look at their walk of shame from my front porch to their car as I closed the door behind me.

Now, I know that Billy defended me, and all, and I really appreciate that, but I knew that he was concerned and disappointed with my behavior. At first he was looking at the floor as I walked in and sat down on my love seat across from him.

He looked up at me in disgust.

"What," I said with a little sass as I wasn't ready for the harshness in his stare.

Billy was surprised with my reaction, which increased his frustration. He may have regretted sticking up for me at that point—I immediately regretted being so gruff.

"I didn't say anything," he said.

"You didn't need to say anything. I can tell."

"I'm concerned."

I didn't have anything valid to say, so I did what any man wearing boxers in his favorite chair would do when he just got left by his girlfriend of seven long wasteful years and was being called on his shit by his best friend—*pout*.

"This is not healthy Matthew. You missed two practices. No one has seen you at school. I know that it sucks, but it's going to spin out of control soon and you won't be able to get this back if you don't change. It's time to dust off and move forward."

I'm not going to lie, as true as that was, I was pissed. I remember thinking: *You have no idea. It's been a week. I mean, Jesus, it was seven years! I'm allowed to have a little destructive behavior for seven wasted years. Right asshole?*

"You don't think I know that?"

"Yes dammit," raising his voice a little. "That's what makes this so hard. I know you know."

He meant well, but I was upset. Upset people are wild cards and you generally don't yell at people that are unpredictable. I just started yelling. It was quite ridiculous.

"I *KNOW*, YOU KNOW, I *KNOW*!"

Billy just yelled back. Why wouldn't he?

"I KNOW!"

We both paused for a moment and thought about what we *actually* said—loudly.

I KNOW, YOU KNOW, I KNOW!

I KNOW!

There's a lot of "knows" in there, not to mention I still looked ridiculous in my boxers; a grown man pouting in his chair. There was nothing else to do now but laugh. So we had a laugh.

"You asshole," he says to me. "Get dressed. Let's go to the game."

I felt really good now—oddly.

* * *

I remember it being very bright outside. It was a normal sunshiny day, but I had been cooped up in my damn apartment for two days. I felt like a vampire out in the sun after that amount of concealment. The grass was soft and still wet from the morning dew as we walked alongside the field to the stands.

There were quite a few people there, way more than attended our games.

Any way, we had a harder time finding Brock and Davy because of the crowd, but Brock didn't let us down. He brought his girlfriend Kathy. That meant there would be drama and a squabble because Brock—well, he's Brock. So, when everyone was sitting down watching the game, Brock said something to piss Kathy off. When Kathy stood up, Brock followed, they irritated the people behind them, caused a mild scene, and we found our saved seats when Kathy bolted off of the bleachers with Brock in tow. That is the drama that is known as Brock and Kathy; could set your watch to it.

"I don't think Brock's going to make it to the diner today," said Billy.

Kathy zoomed past us down the stands. She almost knocked Billy over. I swear I heard him call her an "asshole" under his breath, but there is no evidence to corroborate my accusation so I left it alone.

Brock slipped past us and caught up to her on the side of the bleachers. She stopped as he whispered in her ear. She was still hurt at whatever he said. She crossed her arms as he continued to try and console her.

"She looks pissed," I said.

"He just can't keep his mouth shut," Billy replied.

Davy was having a good time. He was talking to some young, attractive girl he met in the stands.

I was doing my patented temple rubs.

Middle finger-thumb-right hand.

"Oh, my fucking head hurts," I said somewhat quietly to Billy. "God, what is that bright light?"

Billy, the smart ass, looked up into the sky before he said, "The sun."

Touché.

"It seems extra bright today. I need some shades."

We took a seat right in front of Davy and his new "Miss Now."

We're at the game. I want to watch the game. I chanted that to myself hoping that Billy was not going to want to talk. Wrong again.

"So, what are you going to do now," he asks me.

"Watch the game," I said. "Get lunch."

That's what I had planned. I knew where he was going with it. I'm not stupid.

"Right," he said. "That's today's agenda, but what about tomorrow or the next day? What are you going to do?"

"Haven't really thought about that yet."

That was true, I hadn't. I was too busy thinking about how terrible I felt the last few days. I wasn't too concerned for my future. I know he was just trying to help, but you have to *want* to be helped and I wasn't ready yet. I wanted to watch the game at that moment and Billy was distracting me, so I was annoyed.

"You planning on staying in school," he asked me.

"For now," I replied. "LET'S GO B'S!" I thought that might give him the hint, but he continued to pry.

"So what about the *Foxes*? You going to try out?"

They were the closest semi-pro futbol club that I could have tried out for. I always said that I wanted to do that more than anything, but I always had Randy as a crutch holding me back. That was obviously not the case anymore and I know that they expected me to go try out now.

I ignored him and cheered.

"SWITCH! SWITCH!"

I turned to him, annoyed, and asked, "What?"

"The *Foxes*," he repeated. "you going to try out or what?"

I humored him, "Yeah sure. Can I watch the game? Shit! Let's watch the game."

While Billy was trying to be a good friend, one of the women from our home team kicked the ball off one of the opposing members over the end line resulting in a home corner kick.

Explaining what happened next is quite challenging. I like to say that the scene that I'm about to unfold, has changed me. I probably won't be able to forget it, even if I tried. I remember it in slow motion.

There was a corner kick. The ball was placed on the spot and then taken.

She came from what seemed like out of nowhere.

I didn't notice her at first because I was distracted by Billy trying to engage with me.

I know that there were twenty-one other players on that field, but she was the only one that I could see when that play developed. As the ball was sent from the flag, she entered from the opposite side of the field, a perfect run, and left her feet to contact the ball half way. I stood before everyone else in the stands and could only hear my own heart beating. Not only did she have *perfect* form when she contacted the ball with her head, but she wore a delicate pony-tail that bobbed up and down when she ran—it drove me crazy and made my heartbeat even faster.

Suddenly I flashed back—right before my face hit the ground for a second time the other day—I remember seeing that same pony-tail bob up and down as she descended the stairs.

I was positive she sent the ball into the back of the net with her head with more power than I could've kicked it. I was sure everyone in the bleachers erupted all around me, but I was only focusing on *her*. I didn't have time to "cheer" as my jaw dropped. After she scored, she pulled the bottom of her shirt over her head and ran back to midfield. She took her shirt back down and faced the crowd. For a split second, our eyes met and my heart leapt. She finished off her celebration with a bow, and looked back into my eyes for a split second again on her way back up. Her teammates surrounded her like a broken hornets' nest.

Billy had both of his arms around me—shaking me—celebrating that goal. I started hearing the people all around me cheering.

The smile that I wore on my face after that was huge.
Haven't smiled like this in a long time.

* * *

That moment was so surreal; I relived it until the game was over. It was like instant replay in my mind. It was the best goal scored that I had seen *live*, at that point in my life. My bias definitely clouded that opinion as she was so adorable, but a great goal scored nonetheless.

I had to see her. I didn't know how, but I had to. She amazed me.

So we hit *Emery's* after the game and I didn't say anything on the entire walk over there. It was an "emotionally uncomfortable" walk. I couldn't stop thinking about what I saw in the game, so I was half daydreaming; but Brock and Kathy always make people anxious.

Why'd they even come? Brock should've just taken her home when he upset her at the game.

Davy, Billy and I were trying to stay a ways ahead of them while they verbally abused their relationship behind us. We weren't sure if we should slow down and wait for them or to just haul ass and get to the diner.

We hauled ass.

Kathy meant well, but she had an annoying personality and Brock was double the asshole when he was around her—*I know, hard to believe.* We figured they could take the hint and deal with their shit before we got there.

Yeah right.

We were a good 100 feet ahead of them and could hear them, clearly fighting over whatever bullshit thing Brock had said to her.

"I don't understand why you say such mean things," cried Kathy.

"I was trying to be funny, I was out of line. CHRIST! How many times can I say that I'm sorry?"

He said it at the beginning of the game and she still wasn't over it. Yikes!

"What'd he say to her," I asked Davy.

Davy wore a sly grin, "He started out nice by complimenting the color of her mittens…"

"Okay?"

"…he blew it when he said they 'really brought out the color of her nostrils,'" Davy chuckled.

She does have HUGE nostrils…

The guy's an asshole, you can't be that sensitive if you're going to hang around him. He'll smell blood in the water and keep picking at you until you're a drop in the ocean.

So, the three of us get to the diner and do not wait for them. We go in, get a seat, and just wait for them to erupt through the front door.

That didn't happen. They had the "decency" to argue outside the window we were seated at. The glass was vibrating from their shouting.

"Man, I haven't seen them this angry in a long time," Davy opened the discussion.

"Why don't they just break up," Billy replied.

I didn't feel like talking. Davy picked up on it and smacked Billy, it was too early to be discussing break ups. Unbeknownst to them, I was still on a high from thinking about the soccer player.

I decided to throw in my two cents for the hell of it.

"He's scared guys."

"Uh, who's scared," asked a generally confused Davy.

They apparently weren't expecting me to talk. I lowered the menu and looked at them,

"Brock. He's afraid of being alone."

They looked over at him out there fighting with Kathy as I continued.

"He's so afraid that he will stay in his shitty little relationship until she or he finds someone else, because it is *that* scary being alone…and he knows it."

I looked back down at my menu and continued blabbing.

"Enduring a few fights like this over nothing is acceptable because you still have that warm body next to you in bed. Trading off the warmth in your bed over squabbles is not a good barter. Brock understands that. He's the type of asshole that has to endure this shit because he brings it on himself. He's a prick that would set off most girls. They're sensitive and Brock's an insult jukebox. That's just his personality, so he's going to set off everyone he's around. He can't help it, but she has to be the one to end it. He will never leave her because he'll have to start all over again with training another girl to put up with his bullshit. He'd rather endure a daily fight than retrain."

I looked back up at the guys from the menu when I was finished speaking and they both had dumbfounded looks on their faces like I was fucking Buddha or some shit.

* * *

So, after a pretty good high from the game, I was starting to come down a little after watching Brock and Kathy hash it out. It actually should've made me feel a little better about my current situation as I didn't have to deal with that kind of bullshit any more, but I decided to feel sorry for myself instead because I didn't have that bullshit to put up with anymore. It's fucked up, but when you don't want to feel good, you won't.

I got home to an empty, dark apartment and immediately noticed that I had a message on my answering machine. It's hard to miss a lone flashing red light in a dark room.

I'll admit, my heart skipped when I saw it. In the state I was in, you only hope that she's come to her senses and wants to move back in. Deep down I knew that it wasn't going to be her, but there is always that split second of hope from the time that you push the button until you hear the Sith Lord voice through the crappy answering machine speakers.

I walked in, flipped the light on, threw my keys on the counter, pushed the button and began taking off my jacket.

"Hello son."

Damn! Dad.

"It's your dad. You know, the guy you never call any more."

I listened as I poured myself a glass of filtered water from the pitcher in my fridge.

"Your mother and I were wondering if you two were going to come home for Thanksgiving this year."

I spilled some water on the floor, "Shit."

"Love you guys. Give us a call. Goodbye."

I haven't even told my parents yet.

I haven't told anyone really, just my jerk off friends and their significant others. I DID NOT want to call my parents. No one likes to dole out bad news to mom and dad. I was being the selfish one. I didn't want to be the one to have to hear from my parents about how upset the incident makes them.

Not in a, "You're a failure kind of way," but in a "That's terrible, my poor baby boy," kind of way. I was exhausted and didn't want to deal with it, but waiting would only make the dread last longer. I had to suck it up and do it. I grabbed the phone, put my back to the closest wall and slid down until my butt hit the floor. I hit the talk button and got ready to dial.

I shut the phone off. I *really* wasn't ready to talk to them. I did not have *a plan.*

After a few seconds I realized, there is no good way to break this news. You just have to do it. I turned on the phone and dialed immediately before I talked myself out of it again. The phone rang twice and then my mom answered.

Shit. Honestly the only time I can remember that I was upset that my mom answered. She is not going to be able to handle this as well as dad can.

"Hey mom, it's me. You know, I don't think that there is any other way to say this than to just tell you flat out. Randy left me…"

She lost it.

"Now mom, don't…It's going to be okay. You don't need to cry…"

Yeah right. She's my mom. She's going to cry.

"Mom? I can't, I can't understand you mom. Mom? Put dad on the phone, mom, put dad on the phone."

It was like talking to a hyena diagnosed with ADHD. She was bringing me down with her and I was going to lose it. I knew that dad would be concerned, but he was "old school" and I knew he wouldn't allow himself to cry in front of anyone.

"Hey pop. Randy left me…"

He was a little startled, but he was glad that it was legitimate reason as to why mom got upset.

"Yeah, that's why dad…I'm not doing too well it's really hard…It's okay, it's not your fault…I know, I just—I can't seem to believe that this is actually happening. We had plans, you know. Now they're all shot to hell and I have no clue what to do next."

School had to be the next topic as that is of course a major part of my "what to do next." At least that is how dad would see it.

"Yeah, school is okay. I just don't feel like doing anything…I missed a couple days…Yeah, I missed practice too…I know, dad, I know, I'll be okay. I'm glad it's the weekend."

This is where I started getting that pain in my throat again and had to clear it.

"She said she never loved me. I don't know. I don't understand it. Seven years and she hasn't loved me? Why would she stay with me that long…She said that I was unhappy and that she couldn't waste any more time trying to make me happy…She also said that she felt guilty every day that she saw me because she felt it was her fault that I was miserable. I'm more miserable now. I miss her so damn much…Yes I was unhappy, but who isn't…Well, I don't want to be in school. I don't want to be here. I just want to play ball…Well, I'm so close to being done now, I may as well finish…You know, she didn't try very hard with the *happiness*. Can I ask you a personal question? It's really personal dad…Okay. How many times did you and mom have sex on your wedding night?"

It's fucked up to ask that, I know, but I didn't think I'd have a better time to get an honest answer and I needed a point of reference for that area in my life.

I couldn't believe what I was hearing.

"Oh my God. I don't think I've done it that many times in my life…No, she didn't like doing it. I was lucky to get it once a month."

Now he couldn't believe what he was hearing.

"On average I would say we did it once every two, sometimes three, months…Yes, one time…I know, I know…Except on my birthday, then it was whatever…I know, she's cold, she didn't like it when I had to kiss her, she said that it was too rough or that I scared her. From my perspective, I was just sharing with her how into her I was. May have been a little rough, but I really wanted to show her the passion I had. She was very distant and everything was on her terms…mechanical is how I'd describe it."

I remember thinking about what it was like with her.

Okay, take off clothes--

Okay, get in bed--

Okay get aroused--

Okay, insert penis--

Okay, we're done, I must use bathroom right now--

No cuddling.

Ugh, why DID I miss her?

Dad had some more questions.

"Well, I can't really answer that. I tried to get her off every time so that she would like it more, but I don't know if she was faking or not."

I had a hard time with some of the questions.

"She wouldn't let me do that…No, no. I wanted to but she wouldn't let me…She just—she didn't like it with me… Well, my 52-year-old father is getting better sex than me… that's great, but I didn't think it could get any worse, evidently I was wrong…I don't know what I'm going to do. I don't have that much school left. I may as well finish and figure it out from there. I think I want to try out for the *Foxes*."

That was my dad's worst nightmare. They supported me with everything, but I know deep down my dad wanted me to grow up and get a real job. He handled it well.

"Communications, yeah, I don't know, I like to edit stuff, but I'm no reporter…Yeah, I'll be fine. I think rock bottom was a couple days ago so I should be looking up from here; I'm not going to lie, it's still hard. I miss her the most when I sleep. It was nice to know that someone was there with me, even if we weren't intimate…yes *'fucking'* dad. It's going to take some getting used to. I just thought I should let you know that it was only going to be me this year for Thanksgiving…Yeah, love you too pop…Yeah, put mom back on the phone I need to talk to her…Hey mom you okay now?"

She started crying again. I tried to stop her before she started, but I was too slow.

"Please don't cry. I can't talk to you if you're crying… I'm fine, I'll be home next week, you take it easy and don't worry about anything. Everything will work out…I love you too mom, bye."

I shut the phone off and threw it against the wall. I think I broke it. I grabbed one of the pillows on my love seat and started crying uncontrollably—again. It was snot, sweat, and tears like I had never seen it before. I think that was rock bottom. I was wrong when I mentioned that to my dad earlier.

Diligently, Robin sat at her desk working on her homework. Never one to primp for study time, she wore a white tank and practice shorts. She also wore her patented pony-tail that dangled as she typed. Her headphones were on full board, just how she liked it when she studied. Generally she is a Pearl Jam girl, but today she chose the Cranberries. They hit the spot as the words flowed from her hands to the computer. Her eyes, however, were exhausted as she minimized her paper and had an unusual inkling.

Robin launched her web browser and checked the university page. It took some time to convince herself to seek out the men's soccer page, as she read the headlines regarding football and women's basketball, but she hit the tab that she intended to when she minimized her homework. She skimmed over the main article and looked for any storyline regarding the player who received a head injury. There was no mention. Dissatisfied, Robin checked the other hot links and noticed that one of them was the roster. She clicked on the link and was immediately drawn to his image as she remembered "8" was his jersey number.

Matthew Bryerson.

Robin did something next that she probably wouldn't normally do. She hit the online student directory bookmark and plugged in his name. After a few seconds, his address, phone number and email address popped up and she glanced over them. She copied and pasted the information into a word document and saved it to a folder on her desktop: **MATTHEW**.

Satisfied, she popped up her homework and continued to power through.

Suddenly, Robin's eyes were covered with a set of

hands and her heart tried to leap through her chest. In an instantaneous/chaotic motion, she screamed and elbowed the intruder in the groin while pushing herself and her chair over him backwards. Her headphones yanked out of the jack and the chorus to "Zombie" started to blare from the speakers on her system. She screamed through the roll until she caught her breath, and got a good look at the person lying in the fetal position on the floor. It was her friend Max, now struggling to catch his breath.

"Oh my God Max," she stated. "Are you okay? I'm so sorry."

Still struggling to breathe and appropriately contain the pain his man parts were feeling, Max attempted to wrangle out a sentence.

Unable to hear his weep, with an anxious shuffle, Robin turned down her music.

Max, still in a whisper, "I said, I should've known better than to sneak up on *you* like that."

Robin shrugged with agreement as Max sat up and made it to her bed, still cupping his man parts in both hands.

"I am so sorry. You scared the shit out of me."

"Good to know you're prepared. I'll be fine. You didn't hit me that hard actually. I was more startled than anything."

Max paused—still feeling the sting on his dickhead—holding his balls.

"So, what are your plans for the evening?"

Robin hesitated.

"I'm afraid the usual. A little English…A little Math… You know, same old shit."

"What the hell are you doing that for?"

"Well, I would like to better my quality of life by doing well at school, so…?"

"Overrated?"

"Well, not all of us are trust fund babies."

"Okay, I don't have a trust fund-"

"You're never hurting for money…"

"My parents planned."

"We've already talked about this haven't we?"

"Yep."

"Anyways…between practice, the gym, eating, and sleeping—I have to do my homework when I can. That would be tonight."

"You should come out with me tonight and let loose a little," he said wearing his charming grin.

Robin, put on her "shit no" face.

Max was prepared, "No, I will not accept that. Tomorrow is Saturday, you can study then or Sunday even."

"I have to hit the gym and go for a run tomorrow and I have a game on Sunday."

Max picked up Robin and slung her over his shoulder. He was shocked to find she wasn't putting up much of a fight.

"Maaaaax," she whined, semi-reluctantly. "I don't want to go out tonight. I look terrible."

"You're fine."

"I haven't eaten yet."

"Bar food. Stop talking."

He walked through the open door with her over his shoulder, as he pulled the door shut behind him with his right foot.

* * *

Dudley's Pub sat off the street in old town. There wasn't a marquee advertising their business. It was a sportsbar that people just knew to go to. From the street it looked like an abandoned, silent building. As soon as the doors opened, you heard the commerce in the back. There was a front lobby and hostess station—never in use. Out-of-towners were seen standing and waiting in that area for extended periods, thinking that someone would come and seat them. Not that kind of place.

Six shots were lined up in front of the leading lady at her seat at the main bar. Max and four of his flabby cohorts surrounded her. Robin sat and stared at the shots, dumbfounded, speechless, and worried for what was to come. The "fatties" and a trim Max scooped up their shots like a game of jacks and devoured them. One of the "fatties" already had another round of shots poured before their empty shots hit the table. Robin looked at her shot and then looked back at Max for support.

She noticed that Max and the "fatties" were staring back at her, waiting for her to join in so that they can continue their fun—guilt free.

"Max," she whispered, only so he could hear her.

He turned his head closer to hear.

"I haven't eaten yet."

"Come on, it's one shot."

Robin is not amused.

Max ignored her resistance.

"I'll get you a sandwich after you do it."

Like a barge of English soccer fanatics, *Max's Fatties* started chanting, "DO IT!"

"Come on, one shot," he said with a raised voice over the background shouting.

DO IT! DO IT! DO IT!

Robin sullenly picked up the shot and looked at the soda-colored substance.

DO IT! DO IT! DO IT!

"What is this?"

DO IT! DO IT! SHOOT! SHOOT! SHOOT!

"If you need to you can plug your nose. JUST DO IT!"

SHOOT! SHOOT! SHOOT! SHOOT! SHOOT!

SHOOT!

Robin pinched her nose shut with her free hand and threw it back.

SHOOT! YEAAAAAAAAAAAAAAH!

It didn't taste like pop. She gaged a little, but was able to hold it down as she put her head down. Max and the "fatties" watched her quietly, waiting to see that she was okay.

She had them.

"Okay," she coughed. "Where's my sandwich bitch?"

There was a split second of silence. Max was speechless. The short lived silence was broken up by the "fatties" as they picked up Robin by the bottom of her bar stool and heaved her around the room.

The bartender was slightly annoyed, until he saw how many drinks Max had lined up.

"I will need a roast beef on rye to go along with these," Max said to the bartender as he gestured to *all* of the drinks. "Fries, no mayo, extra dijon. Thanks."

Max was accompanied by a server with a tray of their drinks to another table away from the main bar. After the "fatties" tired, they brought Robin, still on her chair, to the table. Everyone dispersed, mingled, and played pool as Robin's rye arrived—ready to be devoured.

Robin was tipsy from the shot she took.

"Drinking makes me so hungry."

Max chuckled.

"You want a beer," he asked.

"I would love one…"

She hesitated, "I've never ordered one before. What should I get?"

"You've never had beer?"

"Stop judging me, I'm a good girl. I get good grades. I don't have time for beer and boys."

After an odd silence, Max gave an uncomfortable giggle and ended it by clearing his throat.

Robin thought about what she said.

"That's sad isn't it," she asked.

"No," he replied with a smile. "Pathetic maybe, but not sad," with a wink.

Robin laughed and punched his shoulder, "Asshole."

Max laughed and signaled the server, "Can I get a Mac-n-Jack and a Long Island Ice Tea please?"

The drinks kept coming as they made their way to the shuffleboard table. Robin didn't realize that she was on her third Long Island. Max felt fine after a shot and two beers. She sent her token down the table as it slid all the way over the edge at the other end without touching any other tokens.

"I am not good at shuffleboard," she stated.

"You're trying too hard," Max replied. "It's called finesse, heard of it?"

"Yeah, isn't that some kind of hairspray?"

Max gave her comment no notice and said, "Just watch me."

He sent a token down the table, gently.

"I've had *way* too much to drink," Robin said. "You know, this is the first time I have ever been drunk….Ever."

"I did not know that," he replied. "That's not a bad thing."

"No," she said. "I'm actually a little proud I have made it this long. Glad we did this though. You were right."

"About what?"

"I *did* need this. Thank you."

Max had a smile while visibly holding back his laughter.

"What?"

"You're *so* drunk," he chuckled.

Robin giggled too, "I am drunk . . . and I don't care."

She took a *deep* sip from her beverage, almost finishing

it, and set her glass down on the table. Robin looked down at the floor and started to cry. Max—now uncomfortable—looked around and noticed that everyone was watching Robin.

"What's the matter?"

"I'm such a boring person," she bellowed.

Trying to comfort her with a hand to her shoulder, "No you're not."

"Yes I am," she said looking up at him now. "I can't even let myself enjoy the moment."

"That's okay," Max said quickly. "You just need to relax."

Robin looked around and noticed the sets of eyes staring at her. She wiped the tears from her face and looked at Max.

"Yes," she replied. "Yes I do."

She picked up what remained from her drink, downed it, and slammed the glass on the table.

"I just need to relax."

They smiled at each other; hers with tear-stained dimples.

"I could use a shot," Max said. "You want a shot?"

"Line 'em up."

They each finished another shot and ended up at the dart board, where Robin was pretty good, throwing a number of bull's-eyes.

"Way better at this than shuffle board," she observed.

Max got up to throw after she pulled her darts.

"So, what else are you good at Robby?"

She started to answer as Max held up his hand, "Besides soccer."

Robin pondered a moment as that was what she was going to say.

"I like to read," she said. "I kickass at Pictionary, and I make great chocolate chip cookies."

"Can you dance?"

"Not really. No."

"Me either, you want to?"

"Yes," she said with a giggle.

"Let's go."

* * *

At *Chucky's Dance Club (CDC)*, Max and Robin danced in a stupor to extremely loud techno music. Robin kept falling over on Max who attempted to keep her upright. Eventually, she fell on her butt, laughing, as Max helped her to her feet and then to another table. The music was so loud that they had to yell directly into each other's ears so they could hear what the other was saying.

"I HAVE TO PEE," he yelled.

"OKAY!"

As Max walked off to the bathroom, Robin sat back and noticed that the lights and the walls were moving in their own circle. She closed her eyes and put her head between her hands, elbows on the table. She took some deep breaths and tried to open her eyes again. She looked at the dance floor and noticed a blur of arms and legs flaying around in their own muffled circles. She closed her eyes again, hands to the head, elbows on the table. A server was at her side, yelling in her ear. Robin turned toward the shout, and opened her eyes long enough to get a good look at the server's face.

"WATER," shouted Robin.

As Max returned to the table, the fast, loud techno sound stopped and there was a lull with slower music as the dancers flooded to the sides of the bar. A few couples lingered, dancing to the slower music, each embracing the other.

"Well, that was fucking interesting," he said.

The server returned with water, Robin took it from her

hand, downing it.

Max, impressed, waits for her to finish.

"Ugh," she gagged, able to control herself.

"Okay?"

She nodded.

"Anyways-" he continued.

"I don't think our server's a woman," Robin interrupted.

A puzzled Max looked at the server behind the bar. *She* had long blonde hair and wore a short black skirt and a tight white top with heels to match.

"Looks like a girl to me."

"Check her neck out when she comes back."

Max watched as *she* approached with another glass of water for Robin.

"Thought you could use another one dear," the server said to Robin, very feminine.

She turned to Max, "Can I get you anything sweetie?"

Max stared at *her* throat the entire time, not hearing the question. Robin gave him a slight slap with the back of her hand, bringing him back.

"I'm fine, thank you."

The server left.

"Good call dude."

They gave each other knuckles without looking.

"This is one interesting bar," said Robin as she was able to look around at the lights without gagging. She took another deep sip from her water.

"Understatement. I just had some guy offer me money to blow *me*."

Robin had a little water come out of her nose, trying not to laugh.

She coughed.

Max handed her a napkin, grinning.

"Are you serious?"

"Yeah," Max said as he looked around the dance floor for the guy that propositioned him. He spotted him at the bar. "He's over there. You can't see it in this light, but his hair is purple."

"How did this happen?"

"Okay, so he used the open urinal next to me and he was like, 'It's loud out there,' and I said, 'WHAT' and we had a good laugh. He said he was drunk and he asked me where I was headed this evening and I told him, 'Home most likely.'

"This is where it got weird.

"He asked me where home is and I told him Nichols Hall and he wanted to know what room. I decided to keep playing along as I began washing my hands and told him '214.'

"He says, 'Shut up that was my room when I was attending' and I was like 'Really?'

"Then he says something like, 'How much? I can go as high as a hundred' and I was like 'What' and he said again, 'How much' so I said 'How much for what' and he was done washing his hands and drying them off as I'm standing there like an idiot and he looks at me and says 'How much money to get you off?'

"I was confused …scared and he goes, 'Orally.' I was walking out the door at this point with my head down and he said something like, 'Call me some time, I etched my phone number on the back of your door.'"

Max and *Purple* made eye contact across the dance floor as *Purple* flashes him the "call me" sign as he lip synced the same thing to Max.

Max smiled and threw him a pity wave.

Robin guffawed.

After the interest of the new bar wore off, Robin and Max headed out the door to walk each other home.

Max had a highly intoxicated Robin slung over his

shoulder as he headed for her dorm.

"I feel so tired," she said. "But I don't want to go to bed yet. I feel like I'll be missing out on something. I feel like I'm flying when I'm on your back."

"No Robby, that's the alcohol on your brain."

After he reached the front of her building, Max set her down gently on her feet. She started to tumble and Max had to steady her with both hands on her shoulders.

"Come on," he said. "I'll walk you up."

Robin started to take out her keys.

"No you can't" she slurped under her breath. "No boys in the dorms. *Shhhh.*"

"Can you make it to your room," he asked her, still with both hands holding her steady.

"I'll be fine."

As she turned to walk away, she fell backward into Max's arms.

"Woe, I'm okay, I just slipped."

"This is ridiculous; I can walk you up to your room."

"Oh Max, don't worry. I'm fine. I'm a big girl."

"A big girl that is *very* drunk."

Robin turned and looked up into Max's eyes.

"I'm fine," she said with a little defiance.

Max kept looking into her eyes.

Robin noticed that he hadn't blinked, once.

"What," she asked him.

She noticed that he had a different look in his eyes and she wasn't sure if she should enjoy it or be concerned by it.

He grabbed her, roughly at first, but it turned into a gentle grasp as he pushed his lips onto hers. Her mouth was open in shock, and then she melted into his deep, soft, wet kiss.

It's difficult to describe any thought *rationally* after the fact when you are deeply upset, because, at the time, you're not *rational*. Looking back and trying to remember how it was that night, after I told my parents, I only know that I did not want to feel that way anymore and I was going to do whatever possible to make that feeling die.

That was my attempt to lessen the blow.

First off, I'm a dumbass and no one should attempt the cra-(wrong word) **stupid** shit I did.

As you recall, I got off the phone with my parents, broke my phone against the wall, and started hugging a pillow like I was going to drown if I let go. Oh, forgot—I was crying a mixture of snot and tears into the cushion as well. So, after what seemed like 30 seconds (*it was really 45 minutes*), I wiped my now wet head dry from the blubbering matter that exuded from my face and–suddenly—I was inspired to check my email. It unfortunately was more of a "hope" that someone actually emailed as opposed to the "necessity" that I have made it sound like.

*Certainly **someone** would email me in this state that I'm in—I mean, God wouldn't want me to kill myself—right?*

Yeah, no emails.

Not even one spam!

Oddly enough, that was so regular, I didn't feel any worse. I don't think that I could've. Thank God for the Internet, and *NO*, this is not heading down that pornographic path that all you horny assholes might think it should have...*I don't know why I didn't think of that. Masturbation might have helped.*

Since the email was a dead end, I knew that I would need a phone eventually so I dug out one of my old corded phones that was still out from the day Randy left. It still worked.

All I could think about was that soccer player I saw. I went to the campus athletic page and started looking for any correlation that I could find. I hit the women's soccer link and found the roster. No dice. It was a shitty picture and there were no individual links.

Webmaster blows!

I checked the recap article.

Eureka!

R. McFarland. Halfway there.

This is the creepy part. I'm like, "There can't be that many 'R. McFarland's' on this campus so...."

....I WENT TO THE STUDENT DIRECTORY AND TYPED IN HER NAME. OKAY.

Robin McFarland.

Address?

Check.

Phone number?

Check.

It even listed her email. Did I write *all* of the information down on a sticky note?

Yep!

Now, what I wanted to do next had not been decided... to be honest, I was just glad I got off my ass and stopped crying.

So, I decided to start crying again, into the same pillow as I sat across from the picture of Robin's profile pic on my computer. I don't know how long I sat there like that, but you always reach a point where you're like, "Okay, 3-2-1 go...."

I think that I was there for another half an hour and I went, "3-2-1 go."

I got up, put on a jacket, grabbed her address information and headed out the door.

I know. Holy shit! What the fuck was I thinking?

Looking back, I can't believe I was not able to talk myself out of doing what I decided to do. There were *so* many variables that were not in my favor. It was past eleven at night and I knew that her dorm would be closed. Even if she was up, why would she come down to see a guy she never met before? Was I thinking of any of this?

Nope!

All I was thinking about was that day I saw her put that ball in the back of the net with her head.

Even if she isn't there, it will feel good to walk past where she lives and know that I might see her outside walking home after practice.

Good to go for a walk anyway. I was sitting on my ass feeling sorry for myself for the past four hours.

I only lived a block away from campus and before I knew it, I realized that her dorm was right around the corner.

Holy shit, I'm actually here. What the fuck n—

I remember hearing two people talking as I came around the front entrance of the building. They appeared to be pretty handsy with each other and when I got a little closer and got a look at the girl it was Robin!

I stopped dead in my tracks and looked around like an asshole to see if there was anyone else who noticed how stupid I looked and felt. Robin and the other guy didn't even notice me. I was like an oak tree on a prairie watching these two interact with each other and then it happened.

They were talking, she looked up at him, there was a pause and then he did what I wanted to do. He laid a massive, supple wet kiss on her face that seemed to last two hours—*it was like five seconds, ten tops.*

I tore back to my house as fast as I could. I remember slamming my door behind me.

Poor door.   It's been getting a lot of mistreatment

lately.

I was right about one thing; I did need my phone again, sooner than later. The unfortunate thing was that it had a short cord and when things like this happen I like to talk and pace. I went to the phone, dialed and waited for an answer.

The phone stopped ringing, but no one said hello.

"Hello....Hello....Hello!"

I was going to panic soon.

"Matthew, how are you," Billy finally replied.

"How'd you know it was me?"

I made the mistake of asking him.

"What other asshole would call me this late? Do you need a ride or something?"

All I could think about was him kissing her.

"She's got a boyfriend man."

"Randy," he asked, and before I could interrupt, "that cheating bitch!"

"No man, Robin. She's got a boyfriend. I was lonely tonight so I looked up her info online and went over to her dorm-"

"Wo, wo, Matt, I just woke up. Who the fuck is Robin and why are you stalking her?"

"She's that soccer chick that scored that header today."

"Oh, she's totally stalk worthy."

"Fuck you. It doesn't matter. I went over to her dorm and she was out front kissing some guy."

"When was this?"

"I don't know. She lives at Owen Hall. I just got back."

"Matt, I love you..."

He gave a deep yawn.

"...but it's past midnight, the dorms are locked up by ten, how else are you going to see her if she wasn't out front tonguing some guy?"

"I don't know," I replied. "I was just sitting here all

alone and felt that I should go and try and see her. I had nothing to lose, except all sense of recent hope."

The conversation started to get very real for me at this point.

"Well, maybe it is for the best right now," Billy said. "The last thing you need is another relationship."

"I just feel so fucking isolated. I hate this. I know you're right, I just feel so lonely and I want to fill that emptiness with the first physical attraction that I see. I'm a fucking mess man. I don't think that I am even ready to start dating again, emotionally any way, but that's all I know and oddly, that's what I want right now to make this feeling go away. I have no idea why it hurt me so bad when I saw her kiss this guy. I don't even know her, but I have already created a scenario in my head where we're supposed to be together."

It was kind of quiet for a while after that rant.

Eventually, Billy spoke up, "Look man. You need to stop beating yourself up. A rebound would be a good thing right now. After that you would probably do well to have a few more rebounds before you look for anything long term."

I knew that he was giving me sound advice, but for whatever reason I was still angry and didn't want to hear it.

"Rebound," I asked him. "The guy who won't fuck his girlfriend is talking about rebounds. Who are you? I can't do one-night-stands. I haven't dated for seven years."

"Matt, you just have to be honest-"

"It's hard to be honest when you can't think of anything to say. Think about it. What do *I* have to offer? 'Hi, I'm Matthew, I'm twenty-five and my girlfriend of seven years just left me because I'm misérable.' Know anyone that would want to date that?"

"I'm running out of things to tell you," he shouted. It took me by surprise and all I could do was listen to what he had to say.

"You have to decide how long you're going to allow the situation that you're in to ruin your life."

Again, there was an odd silence for a while.

I responded with, "All right. Thanks man," and hung up.

* * *

I remember starting to take things in "baby steps." The first one happened when I was randomly out having lunch with Davy. I wasn't saying much, as usual. I was still pretty somber a lot of the time and I didn't feel I had a lot going for me. To make matters worse, Davy decided to drop some news about Randy.

We were sitting in a booth and he was adding sugar to his coffee. He had an interesting way of stirring it, he did it the same every time. He'd tear open the packet, and stir while he dumped it in. He said it mixed quicker that way.

He took a sip and said, "Randy was out with that history dildo from her department."

I finally sat up with some energy.

"Was it Jim or James?"

The second after I said it I knew it was a stupid question, but the adrenaline was flowing. Davy didn't seem to know how to respond to me because he didn't want me to cause a scene, again.

Been doing a lot of that lately.

"Jim or James," he asked me. "Matty, that's the same name."

"Was he the tall, ugly lanky bastard with thick glasses or the short stout guy that talks really fast?"

"They're Jim and James?"

"I know, right?"

"It was the tall lanky one with glasses."

I knew it!

"I knew she had a thing for that asshole. Probably running around behind my back. That bastard came over to our house for dinner. Motherfucker!"

I could tell that Davy was uncomfortable as he looked around and noticed a number of other patrons observing my vulgarity.

Fuck 'em.

It didn't last too long, while he was looking around he sent a wink to someone. He didn't think I noticed, but I did.

"Okay Matty, you need to relax. There are little kids in here. You need to get a phone number. It amazes me how much a new phone number can brighten your day. Watch this."

He got up before I could say anything and started heading in the direction he winked.

I turned and looked and he was already talking to two women sitting in a booth at the other end of the diner. He was probably there for one minute and then he walked back. I noticed he had a napkin in his right hand.

"See this," he said as he waved the napkin around. "This equals this," as he pointed to the smile on his face.

I was impressed.

"How did you do that?"

"I talked to her. I introduced myself and asked her for her number."

"That's it?"

"That's it."

"'Hello, I'm Davy, can I have your number?'"

"Well," he said, "not exactly like that, but basically, yeah."

I didn't feel like that was something that I could do. Davy was good at talking to people, period. I was barely able to talk to people I was familiar and comfortable with.

Strangers? Now that was scary to me.

"I've been out of the game for so long Davy," I said, "I just don't have the balls."

"Every man's got balls," he said, simply.

See, he's really good at talking to people. He knew he was saying the right things to get me off my ass. I really like Davy and *he* knew it.

"I don't know-"

"You got balls. You just need to get to that *point*."

"What point?"

"Well," he said looking like a scientist who discovered a new element, "I call it 'fuck it' point."

"'Fuck it' point?"

"Yes. The point at which your attitude exudes *'what have I got to lose'* and you 'fuck it' and go talk to them."

I hadn't reached that point yet.

"What if they laugh at me?"

Trust me. I knew how stupid I just sounded right after I said it.

Davy was nice about it.

"That's what you're worried about," he asked me.

"It's not just them laughing at me, it's the other people here, seeing me get laughed at. That's hard for me."

"Fuck *them*. First of all, when you do this, you and the person you're talking to are the only two people in the room. If she's mean enough to laugh, fuck *her*, she's not worth your time and you wouldn't want to be with someone that'd do that to you any way."

I had to ponder on those pearls for a moment. I couldn't argue with him. I was starting to grow tired of arguing, which was good.

"You know, you're right. Fuck 'em."

"That's right," he agreed.

"They should be thankful I took the time to notice

them."

"Yep."

"Fuck it."

"Fuck it, Matty. That's all I'm saying."

"I think I'm there..."

"I think you are," he said as he lifted up the number that he got earlier. "Do you want this one, I can get another?"

He made me laugh.

"Let me get my own," I replied.

Without thinking I got up and walked over to a booth behind us that had two cuties in it that I noticed when we got here. I don't remember a lot that happened. I walked up, I talked, she laughed...A LOT. I walked back to our booth (no phone number), as she continued to guffaw.

"What did-"

"Don't talk to me right now."

* * *

It was a game weekend and we were headed to Salt Lake City in the team van, pretty early in the morning. Brock was driving. Davy was sitting shotgun. I was in the seat behind Brock. Billy was sitting next to me. The rest of the team was in the back seats sleeping. I had my headphones on and I was looking out the window.

Billy gave me a nudge with his elbow and I took my headphones off.

"You still mad at me," he asked.

"I was never mad at you," I said. "I was just...embarrassed. I feel really pathetic right now."

"I didn't mean to come off too harsh."

Billy had the ability to make me forget that there were other people in the room. When he was talking to me, I felt that it was always just me and him. He was such a good listener. Sometimes that was good. Sometimes that was bad.

"No, not at all," I continued. "I was just embarrassed--I'm still embarrassed about what I did."

"Don't be embarrassed, you were just trying to move on. It takes time though, I think. You need to just slow down and relax a little."

"Dude, I stalked a girl. I looked her up online and went over to her dorm room...at night. I need to be put in prison or something."

This is where it's bad that he makes me feel like we're the only two here. When we're not.

"Wo, wo, wo," piped in Brock.

Fuck.

"You looked a girl up online and went over to her dorm?"

"Yes," is all I could think to say.

"A random girl you've never met," Brock asked.

I had to give Billy a concerned "here it comes" glare.

"Yes," again is all I could think to say.

"What the fuck were you thinking," piped in Davy.

"Who is it," asked Brock.

"Do we know her," Davy asked.

I gave Billy another "here it comes" look, while shaking my head.

"Now...it's not what you think. I did *see* her before..."

"So it wasn't a random girl," *honestly I can't remember which of those two assholes asked me that.*

"No," I replied. "Can we not talk about this? It's embarrassing for me. I know-"

"So I guess you're moving on Matty," Brock stated.

I could see Davy and Billy cringing at Brock's comment. I calmly replied, "What was that?"

"You're moving on, that's good," he said.

"Brock," pleaded Billy, trying to protect me.

I just protected myself by putting my headphones back on and looked out the window.

"What, you're going to pout now," Brock continued. "Come on. It's a good thing. That's good to move on isn't it?"

I heard him. I acted like I didn't.

"Dude," Davy pleaded with Brock, "just leave it alone."

"I'm pulling for him, even if he is a little creepy, he deserves to get laid just as much as the next guy."

That made Davy chuckle a little. I had to remember that Davy's sense of humor was quite juvenile so I didn't begrudge him. *He probably laughed at the word "laid".*

Billy just looked at me, concerned.

Davy's giggle seemed to spur Brock on.

"I mean, I wouldn't take Matt's approach, but hey, whatever works. I use the Internet for self-loving...I never thought about using it to pick up babies."

I'm the creep? I feel like I just gave the semen-meister a new way to haunt young vulnerable girls.

I turned up the volume on my headphones. Didn't matter, I still heard what he said, even if it was under his breath.

"Don't think I would've told anyone if I did that," he said. "That's one you keep to yourself."

At that point I remember being tired and drifting off to sleep.

I woke up and we had arrived at the hotel in Salt Lake. Brock and Davy were checking us in at the front desk. The rest of us were gathering all of our gear out of the van. Billy took it upon himself to try and "patch up" things so that our stay in small quarters this weekend was not too uncomfortable.

"You know he means well," he said gesturing to Brock. "In his weird kind of way. He's not good at helping people feel better. He'd rather make fun of people."

"He's right in a way," I did believe that when I said it. "What can I really expect? It was a creepy thing I did. If he *didn't* make fun of me, then I'd be surprised."

Billy seemed satisfied with this answer.

"But you know what they say," I continued. "Don't piss off your emotionally-fragile, creepy roommate."

I remember seeing Billy's huge smile grow and I knew he was in.

"What do you have in mind," he asked me.

My smile was bigger than his.

* * *

So, sharing a room with Brock, even for a short period of time, is an interesting experience in and of itself and is different in many ways, depending on his mood.

"God, it's freaking cold in here."

We all knew he was going to be cranky. Brock went straight over to the heater and cranked it all the way to high.

"So turn up the heat," Billy said while unloading his things, not noticing Brock was doing just that.

"What do you think I'm doing," asked Brock.

Yes, I poked the bear.

I took my headphones off and turned the television on, immediately flipping through the channels. Everyone settled in and began watching with me. I took note of this and as soon as something got quasi interesting, I'd change the channel. Davy and Billy didn't give a shit, but I could tell that it was starting to annoy Brock with every time that I did it. After about three times, Brock caved.

"Hey Matt, can we try one channel maybe," Brock didn't yell, but he wasn't quiet either. "Just a thought."

He was sitting behind me and he couldn't see the brief mischievous smile I wore on my face. I had to just hand the remote back to him without looking.

"Thank you," he said.

I took this opportunity to finish getting ready for bed and I brushed my teeth. He changed it to MTV--*ugh, I know.* I finished in the bathroom and hopped into my bed. Billy hopped in the bed alongside me and Davy hopped into his and Brock's. Brock watched MTV the entire time as he undressed to get in bed. He shut off the television and picked up the phone.

"I already set up the wakeup call," I said.

"I'm calling my girlfriend, some of us still have those."

I saw myself jumping from under my covers, tackling him like a lion, grabbing the phone from his hands, and bashing him continually over the head with it.

Instead, I smiled and went to sleep.

* * *

RING, RING, RING

I hate wake up calls; alarms in general really. This morning was different, it was going to be better than Christmas.

Davy was the first to get up, he always was. Same routine. Turn on the shower, pee, get in the shower.

Billy sat up and nudged me. I looked over at Brock, still in bed. I was happy and my face showed it, maniacal as it was. I decided to double check my gear and make sure that it was in order. It was.

I checked it twice last night.

Billy did the same so I didn't feel *too* crazy.

Davy rolled out of the bathroom and Brock started to get up and head into the bathroom, almost unconscious. I have to admit, I panicked; thankfully, Billy didn't.

"Hey Brock," he said to him. "How'd you get the soles of your shoes back to that white?"

I used this brief moment to go back into the bathroom

and use it myself.

Fastest shower I ever took.

As I finished up and exited the bathroom, Brock was headed for the bathroom again, but I needed Billy to take his place. I panicked again, and said the first thing I could think of.

Don't judge me.

"Brock," I squeaked. "I just wanted to let you know that I've never had as much sex as you and your girlfriend have had."

Fucking crickets.

It worked pretty well because Brock stopped in his tracks and looked back at me, giving Billy enough time to sneak past us into the bathroom. He had a raised eyebrow as he looked at me and shut the door. I gulped.

"Okay, buddy. That's....that's okay," is all he could say to me.

I took advantage of the awkwardness and slapped him pretty hard on the shoulder and walked away. It left a red hand print, but he was still so confused by my comment that he didn't even feel it. I was feeling really good now. Everything was working out, and I decided to sing while I was putting on my uniform, "*Moses supposes* his *toeses* are *roses*, but *Moses supposes* erroneously....*" I was going through a show tunes phase.*

Brock was confused and walked over to me.

"What the hell is wrong with you?"

Shit.

"What," I played dumb. "I'm just in a good mood. I can be in a good mood right? I'm telling you I'm really feeling it today. I can feel a couple of goals coming."

I could tell he was still slightly skeptical but Billy was done in the bathroom and Brock grabbed a magazine and head-ed straight for the toilet. He didn't even notice Billy stuffing all of the towels into his bag. When the door closed, the three of us went to town on the room, pulling up all of the sheets, blankets, and drapes.

Very carefully I took Brock's shoes and a sock and placed them in the middle of a barren room for him.

I know, but he had it coming....

Everyone else was ready and waiting for us in the van as we piled *everything* into the back.

We all waited with the two back doors open for him to run out and meet us. We saw the door open and we pulled off.

It's difficult to describe, but he actually put the sock around his twig and bits. He was embarrassed-mad and I think he was going to kill me. I've never seen him run after us so fast. We slowed the van down enough to allow him to keep pace. I dangled (*poor taste in phrasing, I know*) his bag in front of him like a mad man.

"Come on Brock baby! You can do it," I shouted. "Just a little faster!"

"You're almost there," Billy piped in. "Push yourself!"

He was pretty mad, he was running hard for a long time and almost touched the bag, but he had to make sure his sock stayed on.

"You have to do better than that, come on baby!"

"You can do it B," Billy replied. "Just concentrate!"

"I WILL DESTROY BOTH OF YOU!"

I believed him.

"Now Brock, concentrate or you won't get your bag."

"Come on Brock, Push it," Billy echoed.

Though a valiant effort, Brock fell short on the last attempt.

Eventually he slowed, stopped, and hunched over; elbows on his knees.

"See you at the game," I yelled as I tossed the bag out of the back.

"Don't be late," shouted Billy.

I shut the doors of the van as we blasted off to a normal pace.

Our coaches were waiting for us at the field. We stepped out of the van and the coaches made a quick head count. Our head coach naturally noticed that one of our starters was missing, our sweeper no less, and he came up to Davy, Billy, and me. He was a first generation Asian-American, needless to say, English was his second language.

"Where Brock," he asked.

"He should be dangling along soon."

Wink, wink.

Billy and Davy thought it was funny--coach did not.

"Get them to stretch," he replied gesturing to the field.

Poor guy had to rely on *us* as captains.

We got the team geared up, stretched and began running drills. It was right around this time that Brock came around the corner. We started a final lap around the field before the game started. Brock quickly dropped off his things and joined the rest of us as hushed whispers silenced.

Uncomfortable.

We met up with the coaches after a lap and he put out the lineup.

"Brock, you okay?"

"Yeah," he replied to coach. "Warmed up."

I remember the whistle for the start of the first half--and the whistle for the end of the first half. I remember we were down two goals and it was a forgetful performance. Coach was not pleased.

"What in da hell is happening? You guys need to get out there and kick da goddamn ball! If someone hit you, you hit back. They run all over you out there."

Silence.

"No control, no movement, no support. What is

wrong? You guys tired? You need water," he asked grabbing a water jug. "Drink up! We got a lot of water."

I looked up and saw Brock's eyes. He had to be staring at me the whole time, waiting for his moment. He lip synced, "I will destroy you." I had to smirk and shake my head.

"You think this funny!"

Coach snapped me back to reality.

"No coach. I was thinking about something else."

"That's what I talk about, you keep your head in da game. That goes for everyone. We not thinking about da game."

I looked at Brock again and he was satisfied.

I was not.

I remember the final whistle, bent over attempting to catch my breath, Billy beside me, "Yeah, we've had better games," he said.

* * *

The van ride home after a loss is generally pretty quiet. A lot of the guys sleep. I was directly behind Brock as he drove us home—fuming. He broke the discomfort, "I will get you back," looking at me through the rear view.

"As God is your witness Scarlet?"

"What? Fuck you! You think you're so smart with all your movie quotes. If we haven't seen them, your shitty jokes don't work!"

"Dude, that's from 'Gone with the Wind,'" piped in Davy.

"What?"

Brock was taken aback.

"Yeah," Billy replied to Brock. "It's when she goes back home and swears to God that she will work her fingers to the bone to save her land."

Billy turned to me and said under his breath, "I thought everyone saw that."

"Yeah, it was required in my American History Class," I replied aside to Billy.

"Mine too," he said back.

"WHATEVER," yelled Brock. "I haven't seen the fucking thing and I bet half these fuckers in here haven't either."

"Yeah, but they're asleep. Weren't you talking to me?"

"You talking to me," Billy asked—"De Niroesque"—aside under his breath with a snicker.

Davy joined in, "I'm the only one here."

"I know you've seen 'Taxi Driver,'" I said to Brock. "We watched it at your house."

Brock grimaced. I'll have to admit, I had him—but that wasn't enough. I should've stopped. *He's such an asshole though.*

"You know, it's too bad you couldn't reach your bag today Brock. I almost thought you had it, but you just missed it by inches. It's too bad really."

Billy nudged me to get me to stop. Davy turned from the passenger seat and gave me basically the same look. I saw red and kept on. I leaned forward and whispered in Brock's ear, "I was pulling for you."

"THAT'S IT!"

He unbuckled his seatbelt and was on top of me before I could take another breath. I remember feeling a lot of bumps as the van drove off the side of the interstate into the grass separating I-North and I-South. I can only assume that Davy acted quickly, grabbed the wheel, unbuckled and jumped into the driver's seat to save all our asses.

I was in a headlock.

"Apologize!"

I remember gasping out, "Did you forget to take your

medication?"

He tightened his hold around me, "APOLOGIZE!"

Yeah, I bit his arm. He screamed like a girl. This gave me time to maneuver and wrestle with him a bit. He still owned me. He had a huge physical advantage.

"You're such an asshole!"

"PRICK!"

He knocked the wind out of me with his elbow and rolled onto my back. He had me in a Full Nelson.

"I'm gonna kill you!"

He started trying to pound my head into the floor, but I was able to give a little resistance so it didn't hurt as bad as it could. I think we were both really tired, but neither of us had any quit. Billy and some of the other guys started pulling us off of each other. I got kicked in the back of the head by him and that just started everything over. He had two guys on him, but Billy couldn't hold me. I jumped on him and got a lot of clear shots to his head yelling, "You fucking bastard!"

He got loose and the goons-humping-a-football started all over again. I remember others trying to pull us off each other briefly until Davy slammed on the brakes. All of our luggage and almost everyone else flew to the front of the van. Dazed by the shuffle, I remember a rather large hand dragging me out of the side of the van by my hair. I looked over and Davy had Brock in his other hand by his ear. He dropped us onto the pavement sitting next to each other, our backs to the van; on the side of the interstate. He only said one thing, "Fight."

Brock and I made eye contact and we were both embarrassed. The "point" in all of it was gone. Davy wasn't having it though. He was *pissed*!

"FIGHT," he yelled in our faces.

"Wo," I said. "Hey, we don't want to any more all ri-"

He stomped me in the balls. I couldn't breath and my

stomach started aching. That's the worst.

He still had his cleats on.

I was in the fetal position looking up at Brock now.

"What the fuck man," he said as he covered his balls.

Yeah, Davy kicked him straight in the face. Bloody nose, black eyes, lost consciousness for thirty seconds. Davy was serious.

"You're both selfish assholes. Get over yourselves and move on."

I just laid there and watched him walk past a petrified Billy. He got into the driver's seat and fired up the engine.

We eventually made our way back into the van when Brock woke up. Billy sat shotgun now as Brock and I were next to each other right behind them. Davy had the rear view mirror on us the rest of the way home, with the occasional judgmental glare. I had ice on my balls. My stomach was still hurting. Brock was slouched next to me with gauze from the van first aid kit up both nostrils.

Brock turned to me, "You done with that?"

I grimaced and handed the ice pack to him, "Yeah, here."

He took it and put it straight on his nose and forehead.

Billy looked over at Davy, "So do you think they're going to have cute kids?"

Davy laughed.

Billy smiled.

Brock and I sat in pain.

"Fucking assholes," Brock gasped under his breath aside to me.

"Dicks."

After a brief and satisfying moment, Max released her. As he pulled away, a very stunned Robin got a whiff of his breath, holding an after taste of onions and stale beer in her mouth. Her expression was "drop-jaw, speechless."

His was "enthusiasm."

As abrupt as the kiss was, Robin started to feel the consequences of the evening stir inside of her for a moment. She looked up at him and released a waterfall of cocktails, beer, and whatever was left of her roast beef and rye all over his face, shooting it right into his eyes, mouth and nose sopping down the front of him; knocking him to the ground.

Max began spitting/vomiting, as he started to wipe the remains from his eyes with a whiny cry of disgust. Robin turned and quickly unlocked the door and headed up to her room.

"Robin, wait!"

The perimeter door slammed and locked shut behind her.

* * *

BEEP! BEEP! BEEP! went her alarm clock. Robin sat up in her bed with morning eyes and started to rub her temples with both hands. *BEEP! BEEP! BEE-* she yanked the cord from the wall. She gave a tortured moan. She stepped out of bed, woozy, and b-lined it to the bathroom. There was a lot of moaning and heaving. She left the bathroom, looked at her bed and noticed even more vomit on her pillow and blankets. Disgusted, she grabbed the bedding, wadding it into a pile. She grabbed her full dirty laundry basket, was hit with a whiff of stench, dropped the basket, and ran to the bathroom for Ralph-

Fest round two. Once the heaving was completed, she picked up her dirty clothes, determined to get to the laundry room; holding her breath. When she got there, she immediately loaded a machine full of her bedding and laundry soap. Dizzy and spinning, she retched right into the laundry machine all over her already filthy bedding. She shook her head, closed the lid and started the machine. She placed the empty laundry basket on the dryer and turned to exit-

Startled; Robin was ambushed by what she calculated to be the rest of the people on her floor, eyeing her. She cleared her throat, feeling the blush come on.

"Late night, last night," is all she could think to say as she walked out past everyone—feeling their eyes on her back —returning to her room.

She pulled a bottled water from her mini-fridge and dropped two aspirin. She sat on her bed, finished the water, laid down and rolled into the only clean blanket she had left, drifting off to sleep.

RAP! RAP! RAP!

Robin felt like she just reached sleep when the knocking persisted. She sat up with a heavy headache.

RAP! RAP! RAP! RAP! RAP! RAP! RAP! RAP!

"Robby," said a muffled Missy through the door. "Are you okay? I talked to your RA, she said you were a little sick."

With closed eyes, Robin made her way to the door. She unlocked and opened it a crack, turned, and headed back to bed. She fell like a domino and pulled the lone blanket over her head.

"Missy, I had way too much alcohol last night."

Missy habitually flipped her light on.

"No, please," said Robin. "No lights."

"My God you're hung over. Tell me what happened."

Robin suddenly pictured Max falling to the ground, drenched with the chow that she sent his way the night before.

"I don't really remember what happened."

"You didn't wake up next to anyone you didn't recognize did you?"

"Just my hangover," Robin said with a smile. "I went out with Max and his friends last night-"

"Max, he's cute."

"We did some shots…of what? I don't know. We played pool, darts, shuffle board, another shot. We went to *Chucky's* and tried to dance a little, I think. He walked me home."

"That is a rough night of drinking Rob," said Missy. "You should've gone with me first. No shots, I would've eased you into it. I wouldn't want you to hate it."

"No one made me do anything."

Suddenly Robin remembered sitting at the bar with Max and ALL of his friends chanting, *SHOOT, SHOOT, SHOOT!*

"It was fun--until I got sick," she continued. "Then it became *un*-fun."

"Did you throw up in the washer," asked Missy.

"Yep."

"Well that's nothing. The first time I got sick drinking I..."

Robin tuned her out as she continued with her story. She started to day dream about Matthew playing soccer. She remembered him lining up in the wall and getting struck in the head with the ball in slow motion as Missy tugged on her shoulder.

"Robin, are you listening to me?"

"No...I mean yes...what were you saying?"

"You need to get some food....and water. Lots and lots of water."

"Missy, I just want to sleep. I have *so* much homework. I'm going to kill Max."

"Let's just get to the cafeteria and get you some eggs and toast and see where we're at."

Robin sat up with a sigh, her head felt like a box of rocks on her shoulders.

Missy took in a whiff of her. The aroma almost made her gag.

Robin lifted her arms and smelled her armpits.

"I'll go down, but I need to switch out my laundry first."

"Go shower and brush your teeth--not in that particular order," said Missy, holding back a gag. "I'll get your laundry."

* * *

Robin sat at her desk, typing another paper. She stopped to daydream. Being as she was extremely bored, she minimized her paper and popped up Matthew's personal info file. She picked up her phone and dialed his number, almost without thinking.

BUZZZ....

1 ring....

BUZZZZ....

2...

BU-

Robin panicked near the third ring and hung up. Almost without thought again, she wrote down his address on a sticky note, slipped on her coat and walked out the door. She felt confident while inside the dorm, walking through the halls, and out to the front of the building.

Thoughts of the first time she saw him filled her head again as he stood bravely in the wall. She giggled a little when she pictured the ball smashing into his face. Part of the giggle was the excitement of possibly talking to him--hell it could go well and they might see each other again. Part of the giggle was the simple fact that shit is funny when people get hit in the head with stuff too.

Before she knew it, she was rounding a corner and checking the address on the paper when she noticed *him* entering his front door. He closed it behind him as she stepped in front of his walkway and paused to muster her courage, staring at the door. As she waited, thinking about what she might say, she didn't notice a car pull up and park out front, behind her. A woman exited the car. Right as Robin started heading toward his door, the woman that exited the car walked around her like she wasn't even there, heading for Matthew's door as well. Robin noticed her as they arrived at the door at the same time.

Panic.

"Oh, 112," Robin said. "Oops, I need 115," with a forced giggle as she walked off.

The woman expressed concern and confusion on her face. She looked away from Robin and knocked on the door.

Robin sneaked around the corner and peered to see what was happening.

There was an answer at the front door and Matthew appeared excited to see this woman as he gave a hug that lifted her a little off her feet and then kissed her cheek. They conversed, but it was muffled. They went into the apartment. Robin quickly moved to the window and stood on her tiptoes to see what unfolded. As they talked, Matthew started to yowl. The woman consoled him with a hug that he hesitated to return--at first. He gave in and continued to bawl into her shoulder. At their embrace, Robin was struck with jealousy. She wondered why he was in pain, who that woman was, and wished that *she* could be the one to comfort him.

Robin saw tears emerge from the woman's eyes now.

She started to tire on her toes as her chin came down against the window. Instinctively, she knew it was a loud noise that she made as she turned to the right with her back to the wall. Looking up and to the left out of the corner of her eye,

Robin noticed his shadow peering out the window to see if anyone was there. She imagined his tears looking forward alongside her and what a pair they would make right now, immersed in their angst—silhouette. His shadow retreated and Robin felt like she could breathe a little easier. Moments passed as she continued to breathe deeper. She turned left on her hands and knees and found her face inches away from a teeth-baring Chow with a growl. Though her heart kicked-the-shit-out-of the inside of her chest, her body did not move—other than the widening of her eyelids. She slowly backed up on all fours; the dog's growl became louder with every sound that she made. Robin's tactile senses came to the forefront of her mind as she felt the pavement graze her kneecaps-the inside of her hands scraped and scratched ever slowly. The natural tension from her fear started to make her shoulders and gluteus cramp as she continued to back away.

Believing the distance to be safe enough for a jolt, she jumped right, losing consciousness to the-

PING!

* * *

SLAM!

Robin sat up like a mousetrap, shivering. She looked down and noticed the Chow was cuddled up and wrapped in her legs. Unaware of how long she'd been there, she put both hands to her temples and started to rub them, moaning. The dog got up and walked away.

"Rough night?"

Robin turned and the woman from Matthew's apartment was looking down at her from his front stoop.

"Yeah, kind of cold," she replied.

"You have a pretty nasty gash on your forehead."

Robin investigated and grimaced when she touched it.

She checked her watch.

"Shit! I have a game today."

Robin stood and walked away.

"You should get that cleaned and looked at," the woman shouted to her as she started to jog off now.

She didn't hear her.

She looked down and noticed the Chow, playfully barking and running alongside her.

* * *

In her dorm room, Robin washed out the gash on her forehead with a damp washcloth. She dried off the now scab with a hand towel and hopped into the shower.

* * *

On an extremely wet Sunday afternoon, Robin showed up to the field and began to put her cleats on. She was wearing a white bandana across her forehead. She looked to the stands, hoping she'd see Matthew there. There were three--maybe four--sets of parents all bundled up in blankets and raincoats. Robin continued with her warm up routine, stretching, jogging and drills as she continually peered over at the stands to see if Matthew had come. A referee approached her as she was passing a ball back and forth with one of her teammates.

"Miss, I'm afraid you are going to have to take that off."

Robin was not paying attention to her partner or the ref. She saw Matthew walking over to the bleachers. She had a huge smile on her face and her chest started to warm the inside of her belly as she had a slight blush.

"That bandana is not part of your uniform," the ref said.

Robin continued to watch Matthew walk through the more heavily filled stands and take a seat on the bottom row just off midfield. Robin didn't want to look away.

"Miss? MISS?!"

Robin was shocked as she came to and saw the ref standing in her bubble.

"You can't wear that," he said, pointing to her forehead. "It's not part of the uniform."

Robin took it off. She wore a large white square bandage covering the wound on her forehead. Satisfied, the ref left. Robin resumed drills. She gave one last glance over at Matthew, who appeared bored, leaning back against the bleacher a row above him, yawning. The home clock showed twenty seconds to kick off as the coach called them in for a final conference. The announcer began calling out the visitor's lineup as Robin and her teammates prepared for their name's to be called. They got into a line, each with a university women's soccer t-shirt for someone in the crowd. The announcer read off the home lineup and all of the starters crossed the field and began throwing their t-shirts into the crowd. Robin struggled with what to do with hers because Matthew was sitting too far away. She threw it as hard as she could, but closer fans in the crowd snatched it out of the air.

A whistle and the ball was kicked off. The home team aggressed the ball down the field and was rewarded with a corner kick on their first possession. The ball was crossed. Robin went up for it. Robin had a brief moment of elation as she left her feet, thinking that she was high enough to get the ball, then she felt a body hitting her legs from under her in midair. She came down on her left shoulder—then neck.

Matthew stood.

The whistle stopped play this time as the trainer rushed onto the field.

The ref pulled a yellow card from his pocket. The crowd gave a mixture of cheers and boos as some felt a red card was more suiting.

Robin had the wind knocked out of her. She watched the faces float above her as they gave instructions. It sounded like her ears were under water. Her breath wriggled back into her lungs and the speaking faces were less muffled now.

"I can stand," she gasped.

She was helped to her feet. The trainer quickly put an ice pack on her shoulder and neck.

The crowd applauded.

Robin made her way off the field. She sat on the bench as the trainer started to massage her shoulder. With a scowl she looked for Matthew.

She didn't see him.

* * *

Hours later Robin sat in her chair in her dorm; a wreck. Her forehead still had a bandage right on the middle of it, and she was wearing a neck brace she was given after her visit to the emergency room.

Missy entered her room without knocking and stood right in front of her as Robin looked up at her. Missy treated her like a painting without saying anything.

Robin waited for her to speak.

"It could be way worse."

Robin didn't say anything.

"What happened to your forehead?"

"Uh," Robin paused, unready for that question.

Missy's rudeness rescued her again, "Before you say no, hear me out. I think you could use a drink."

Robin just glanced at her, defeated.

"You know you could use a drink."

"Missy-"

"Don't be embarrassed. Use it. It's...it's a conversation starter. People are going to wonder. Let them ask...."

Missy continued to blabber. Robin was tired and wanted to be left alone, but she was also tired enough to give in. She stood, grabbed her jacket and opened her door. She turned her body to look at Missy, raising her eyebrows in the "Well?" position.

Missy stopped talking and looked at Robin.

Missy quickly walked out the door in front of Robin before she could change her mind.

Robin followed, shutting her door behind her.

* * *

It wasn't long after they arrived that Robin found herself in the restroom. Missy was busy talking to people other than Robin and although she did need to relieve herself, she was breaking up the boredom of watching Missy socialize.

Dreading her exit from the restroom, she took her time washing and drying her hands. At the mirror she looked at her bandage and neck brace and couldn't believe she found herself out in public like this. Rather than cry, she decided to leave the bathroom and let Missy know that she'd have an early evening. She didn't think that Missy would mind as she had plenty of people here to entertain her.

She walked past a table and was flagged down by the woman she met on Matthew's porch that morning.

"My God, what happened," she asked.

Robin quickly positioned her body and checked each member of the party to see if Matthew was present. He wasn't there.

"Hi," she replied.

The woman extended a light hand to her shoulder from her barstool and turned to her party, "I found her on the ground outside Matty's apartment this morning."

The three of them lifted their eyebrows to her.

"What happened to your neck?"

"Is Matthew here with you guys?"

"You mean *Jafar*," asked the tall handsome one.

Everyone laughed except Robin.

"Yeah," said the one with the shaved head.   "He's around here somewhere."

Robin turned herself around, now frantically searching for any sign of Matthew, not wanting him to see her like this. She eyed him leaving the restroom as he headed over to the bar. She turned away and saw Missy heading her way. There was a sudden sense of claustrophobia that clouded her as she looked down at the floor.

"Robin, who are these guys," Missy asked.

Missy inserted herself in between the tall handsome one and the woman. She smiled at the tall one as he grinned back. Robin turned herself again, seeing that Matthew was still at the bar, bored, waiting for his drinks.

"I'm Missy."

"Davy," as he shook her hand.

Missy looked over at the shaved head and the short guy. The short guy nudged "shaved head."

"Huh, oh Brock," extending his hand.

"Billy."

"I had no idea Robin had such cute friends."

Billy, Brock and Davy give a "Who the fuck is Robin?" look to each other.

"So what happened to your neck," the nameless woman asked her, again.

Robin felt the onset of a panic attack as she watched Missy flirt with the boys. She turned herself one last time and saw that Matthew now had a tray of drinks on the bar, counting them. Robin felt her own heart pounding very rapidly now as Matthew started to head her way.

Missy's flirty laugh cleared her mind.

"Missy? My neck is really hurting. I need to go back and take some of my pills."

Missy smiled at Davy and Billy as she helped Robin walk away, "You don't have any pills," she whispered.

"I'll explain later."

Robin and Missy exited out the front door as Matthew set the drinks on the table.

* * *

"Okay," said Missy as Robin's door swung open. "Please tell me what happened back there."

"They were Matthew's friends."

"Who's Matthew," asked Missy.

"Some guy I've had an unhealthy obsession with lately. He's the guy that got hit in the head with the ball at the game we went to a few weeks ago."

"That could've been a great opportunity for you to meet him."

Robin was at the brink of tears.

"Right," she started. "I should've said, *'Hi, my name is Robin. I'm obsessed with you, I stalk you, like the gash, oh, my neck hurts too!'* Robin started to cry. "I don't know, maybe it's just me, but I don't feel too attractive right now."

Missy couldn't think of anything to say and her face was empathetic.

"I think that woman was his girlfriend any way."

"At the bar?"

"She was over there with him last night when this happened," Robin said pointing at her forehead.

"Did you see them kiss," asked Missy.

"They hugged, he gave her a kiss on the cheek."

"They're not dating."

"Okay, good. I didn't think so either but it's good to

hear someone else that's not crazy say that."

Robin wiped away the tears and started to smile at Missy who giggled.

"How'd you get that gash on your head?"

Robin gives her an uninspired look, but knows now that she has to tell her the story.

I remember that my walk still had a hitch in it when Beth came to visit me. I waved goodbye to those assholes when they dropped me off. They didn't deserve a wave, I suppose, but some things just become habit. I unlocked my front door, carried in my stuff, set it immediately on the floor and sat myself in a chair. Though there was still a sting on my dick-balls, I didn't feel like shit/vomiting anymore, so I had that going for me. I remember thinking that I needed a shower when there was a knock at the door.

Tired and not expecting anyone, I was a little annoyed--then I opened the door and saw my sister and that made things better.

"What?!"

My sister rarely makes house calls, so I always try and let her know that I appreciate it. I love her. She's the best. I'll have to tell her that someday, but until then, being excited to see her will have to do.

I gave her a big hug and a kiss on the cheek.

"Get in here."

"So, mom told me."

"What?"

Oh shit, I forgot about Randy.

"Randy," she said, just as I thought it.

I was overwhelmed—I lost it. My sister checking on me at my house pushed a fragile man over. I couldn't stop sobbing. Tears and snot all over again. Those fluids were on Beth's shoulder before I could blink.

"I miss her," I cried. "I know it sounds weird because she was such a downer to everyone but I do miss her."

She didn't say anything. She didn't need to. Randy and Beth were indifferent. They didn't dislike each other, but they weren't buddies either.

It was uncomfortably quiet when there was a clack at the window. I thought a bird flew into it. I went to check but didn't see anything. I was glad there was something there to change the subject, even if it was brief.

"We can sit down," I said wiping my nose.

Beth took a seat at the table, I sat across from her.

"So, how was your weekend," I asked.

"It was okay," she said with a giggle.

PING!!!!!!

I went to the window to investigate the odd sound again, but there appeared to be nothing.

Weird.

I decided to make some hot chocolate while we were talking.

"You going to mom and dads for Thanksgiving," she asked me.

"Yeah, I committed to Dad over the phone. No backing out now."

"It'll be good to see the family."

"Yeah."

"I think you should surround yourself with people that genuinely care about you right now. It'll help."

"Sure."

The tea pot whistle sounded. I got the cups ready and poured the water.

"So what are your plans now," she asked me, stirring her cocoa.

"School."

"And then what?"

"Haven't thought that far ahead."

She took a slow, loud sip of her cocoa.

"When are you going home?"

"I'll be there Wednesday night, I have school in the

morning."

We both took a sip at the same time. Slow. Loud.

Weird.

"It's going to be weird not having her there. She's been a part of my life for seven years."

Yeah, I made it weirder with that comment.

"Well, we'll try and make it as comfortable as possible."

I took a deep breath.

"What," she asked.

"I'll be okay hanging out with you and mom and dad, but everyone else is going to annoy me."

"Well you don't have to be around anyone that you don't want to."

"I just hate having the pity eyes on me, all day."

"Aren't you used to that by now," she laughed a little harder than she should've.

It did make me smile though.

"You're an asshole."

She laughed harder.

"I'm really glad you came over to see me."

I was.

"You're my little brother and I love you."

"I really appreciate it. I know how busy you are."

"Speaking of which, I have to take off really early tomorrow morning. I'll be back in the afternoon."

"I'll be up a bit. You can sleep in the bed if you want."

"Are the sheets clean."

Another smile.

"Pathetically," I replied. "Yes, they are."

"Well good night," she said. She stood and gave me a kiss on top of my head. "We'll do something tomorrow night."

I had another sip from my cocoa as she went to bed. I decided to check my email. You never know.

Yep, nothing.

I turned the TV on. I flipped through the channels, I just liked the noise. I think I stopped on an infomercial, I can't remember. I was thinking about life after Randy.

LAR.

I fell asleep thinking about her smile...

I woke up to mild mumbling out my front door. My sister was talking to someone. I decided to get up as she appeared to be shouting now. I opened the door and stepped out beside her.

"Who are you yelling at?"

"I don't know, some girl."

"Okay," I said with a yawn. "I'm going back to bed. I'll see you later."

* * *

"Yeah, my sister's in town."

KNOCK.

The door opens.

It has to be Beth.

I gave her a side hug as she entered.

"That sounds like fun," I said into the phone.

Billy.

"We could probably meet you there in an hour," I double check with my sister.

She nodded.

"Dudley's in an hour sounds great."

CLICK

"How was your day," I asked her.

"Busy. You?"

"Boring. That's going to change though. Have you met Billy yet?"

"I don't think so. When would I?"

"I don't know, but he's fun. Don't turn your back on

him though, he'll down your drink when you're not looking."

"Your *friend* does this?"

"He's frugal."

"Dad would love him."

"Yep."

* * *

I remember Billy carrying a tray of our drinks back from the bar as Beth was in the middle of telling Brock and Davy my most embarrassing childhood story.

"Wait, wait, wait, start over, I want to hear this," he said as he set the drinks down and took his seat.

The rest of us grabbed our drinks.

"It's not *that* good," I remember lying.

"I don't care," Billy replied.

"So," she continued. "When Matty was about eleven (she checked with me and I gave her a nod) he was apparently very bored—at least I hope he was—and he was told he had to clean his room. He found one of those glass, 12oz Mountain Dew bottles; you know, the ones with the small head and large, cylinder body."

"Yeah, the little green ones," Brock piped in.

"Yes. I don't know what he was thinking, but he decides to see how large the hole on the end of the bottle was. He didn't use his fingers. Yeah, he put his dick in it."

Laughter and looks in my direction as expected.

"Technically I was measuring the girth of my penis, but continue."

"There's more," Billy asked through laughter.

"So this bottle is stuck around his weenie and he cannot yank it off—pun intended..."

She's hilarious.

"...this bright boy sitting next to me sneaks into the

kitchen to get some butter to see if he can lube it off, right? He ends up with a *cube* of butter in his bedroom and starts 'corn-cobbing' his dick, but, it gets worse; he starts getting '*moved*' and the ring gets tighter."

Giggles are now guffaws.

"Now he's losing circulation."

I felt their eyes on me as I looked down, to take a drink. They were still laughing, but waiting for a response.

"It hurt really bad," I said to the jackals.

SNORTS

"So he's moaning/crying and mom hears it."

"Oh shit," shrieks Davy.

"She checks on him and he had his back to the door, but her entrance startled him and he turns to face her."

CRICKETS

"There is a green bottle hanging from his purple boner and a cube of butter in his hand. I shit you not, my mother fainted."

ROARS

"She did," I stated, sipping my beer.

"She eventually came to and rushed Matty to the hospital. They were there for about four hours."

"My mom didn't look at me or talk to me for a month."

"We called him *Jafar* after that."

"Inside Joke," I stated.

"*Jafar*? Why that," Davy asked.

"We couldn't call him jug fucker, like we wanted to."

More laughter.

"We coded it *Jafar* instead. It made our viewing of *Alladin* twice as funny I can assure you."

"I'm *so* glad you could make it here to see all of us," I chaffed.

"I *am* glad you came," Billy giggled.

"Me too. I'm buying you a beer," jeered Brock.

I had to pee, so I did. I heard my sister say, "I think he's mad at me," as I stepped away. I wasn't. Just a little embarrassed. I was glad she was here.

When I was done in the restroom, I went to the bar to get drinks. I noticed two girls had joined the party. Beth was engaged with one of them, Davy was frolicking with the other.

The drinks took quite a long time and when I finally got over there, the girls were gone.

"Okay, I got beers, shots, wine, and no money, who's paying me," I said as I set the drinks down on the table.

Brock and Davy gave me some cash.

"I'll get you later," said Billy.

"Nice," I replied.

"What? I will."

"Sure you will," piped in Brock. "We know you will."

"Yeah," said Davy.

Beth just smirked at me.

* * *

Beth and I skipped home that night—*well skipped as well as drunk assholes skip*—I remember singing "Come to My Window" by Melissa. It's a fun song to sing when you're drunk...

I had a hard time unlocking the door, but we made it through.

"Take me drunk, I'm home again," I said.

I always say that. It's annoying, I'm sure.

My sister said what she always says, "No shit."

I remember putting-no-throwing my keys on the coffee table and face-planting onto my love seat.

"I went over my well limit this time."

"Yes you did," she said. "I think you should take some ibuprofen."

"Shit, that's a good idea."

I got up and did that....I think. Either way, I ended up at the love seat, "I'm sleeping here, you be good to my bed."

"Good night."

I was snoring before she said it.

Robin opened her eyes as she laid in her bed. She had on her neck brace and the Band-Aid was still on her forehead. She sat up, pulled her brace off, massaged her neck and shoulders, and put the brace back on as she got up from her bed and went out into the family room of her parent's house.

It was silent.

Robin looked at the clock and noticed that it was 7:30 in the morning. She went upstairs and headed over to the coffee pot. There appeared to be a couple of cups left and it was still warm to her touch. She was pouring herself a cup when her parents walked in the back door through the garage carrying many bags of groceries. Robin turned her body around and began to head over to her mother and father with her arms open for a hug...mom handed her two grocery bags.

"Thank you Robin," said mom. "It was a madhouse at the store today."

Her dad handed her his bags too as she struggled to hold everything. Dad escaped back out to the car.

"There are a lot more groceries out here honey," he said. "I could use your help."

Mother continued talking as she took off her gloves and coat and placed them in the closet.

Desponded, Robin headed for the table and set the groceries down, and took a seat.

"I could not believe how rude the checkout person was," said mom. "I know that it is busy and stressful at this time of year, but my God, do they really need to throw our groceries down the checkout like they're pinballs? I don't think so. I had a loaf of bread that was packed in the bottom of a bag with chips laying on top of them. I know that chips are light, but bread *always* goes on top—that's common sense..."

Mother finally noticed Robin's neck brace.

"What happened to your neck?"

Robin sighed at the superficial comment.

"What's on your forehead? That looks hideous. How long do you have to wear that?"

Her father came back through the door with another load of groceries. He set them on the table and looked over at Robin, "Hey, what happened to your neck?"

Mother and father were silent—waiting for her answer.

She looked at them, went down to her bedroom, and slammed the door.

Mom and dad looked at each other—confused.

THANKSGIVING AFTERNOON....*EFFING YAY!*

Robin laid awake with her neck brace on staring at the ceiling. Robin followed her morning routine—brace off, shoulder rub, rotate head, brace on, robe on over her PJs, and opened her bedroom door to a beehive of relatives mingling and eating. Everyone turned and noticed her as the buzzing stopped. She retreated to her room, slamming her door behind her. The clock on her nightstand read 2:30!

Robin put on her foundation makeup, careful not to touch the bandage on her forehead and pulled on whatever pants were closest. She brushed her hair without a mirror and threw it into a pony tail. She took off her neck brace in order to take her PJ top off and threw on a "clean" shirt. Brace back on, she took a deep breath and exited her bedroom. The buzzing stopped as everyone took a quick look this time and then back to buzzing again.

Not one "hello."

Robin slammed her door behind her unnoticed by the bees. She headed to the main buffet style table, grabbed a plate and started dishing up food. Robin didn't notice her grand-mother behind her in line.

"What happened to your neck dear?"

"Hi grandma," said Robin, setting her plate down and giving her a hug. "I hurt it playing soccer."

"Such a rough sport dear," grandma and Robin contin-ued to walk down the line, filling up their plates. "I don't know why your mother let you pick that up."

"Well, grandma, I love it so mom really didn't have a choice."

"Well, if you like to abuse yourself, you have no one to blame but yourself."

"Well, it's just part of the game and that game has brought me a scholarship so it is worth the bumps and bruises to me...." Robin trailed off as she turned to look at her grandma who had already left the buffet line.

Robin located a seat at a desolate table as she ate her meal alone. People were actively engaged with each other in their own small conversations all around her. No one sat down to talk to her while she ate.

Over time, the conversations began to move into other parts of the home and Robin ended up alone in the same seat. She rolled a black olive across her plate from one side to the other. She looked up at the clock and saw that it was 6pm.

Robin punctured the olive on her plate with her fork and plopped it into her mouth. She got up from the table and went into the family room where everyone was playing board games.

As Robin made her way through her family members, they began to engage with her and she wished she would've stayed in bed.

"Do you shower with that thing on," asked her flannel-wearing/handlebar-mustache uncle.

She didn't know what to say to him so she stared, confused.

"Does it itch," asked her coke-bottle-glasses-wearing aunt who was pointing at Robin's neck.

"No," she replied, knowing that this is how her evening was going to go.

The next question came from her mid-life-crisis aunt with very poorly frosted blonde hair worn in a shiny perm. She had fake boobs that her shirt made sure everyone knew that simple fact in case they missed it, "Do you get a lot of sympathy from the men wearing that thing? I might get one," as she laughed at herself while adjusting her boobs in her bra.

Again, Robin couldn't think of anything to say to that?

She was approached by her very tall, formal uncle that wore a black suit and tie. Looking down at her, "Does that get in the way when you're making out?"

"I don't make out with anyone, currently so..."

He chuckled with a louder bellow than Robin's comment deserved.

Robin frowned at him.

He laid a hand to her shoulder, "You'll find someone someday."

He walked off, continuing with his loud chortle.

Robin just rolled her eyes.

"Do you have amnesia?"

Robin didn't even recognize that relative and they were gone before she could answer.

The next set of questions seemed to all happen at once. Robin either had nothing to say, or was not allowed to say anything before the persons asking the questions lost interest and walked off.

"Are you dating anyone-"

"Do you always wear your hair like that-"

"Have you gained weight-"

"Why don't you ever call me-"

"Call me-"

"Just call me-"

"Call me-"

CALL ME! CALL ME! CALL ME!

DING-DONG!

The front door swung open. Robin turned to look and was thankful for the distraction. Her older brother, Cal, walked through the front door and was bombarded by all the family members that were previously interrogating her.

Cal appeared happy to finally be home as he hugged each family member that was in line, fawning over him.

Robin stayed where she was, looking over at him.

As he hugged one of his aunts, he looked up and made eye contact with Robin.

She smiled.

Cal smiled back for a moment and then started answering questions that the crowd had for him.

Robin retreated to a secluded room and sat on a love seat. She started to wipe her face downward with both hands-

"Hey big sis."

She looked through her hands at her big brother and smiled.

"Did I miss the dust settling," he asked her.

"Just in time," she replied as she stood up to hug him.

Robin sat back down. Cal grabbed a chair and sat across from her.

"When did you get into town?"

"Yesterday," she replied. "I stayed the night."

"How are Doreen and Chester," he asked with a devilish grin.

"*Mom* and *Dad* are…well…mom and dad."

"Yeah, what the *HELL* happened to your neck?"

That gave her a giggle.

"My head traded places with my feet in under a second."

"What did you learn?"

"That I care too much."

He returned a giggle for Robin.

"How long are you going to be off the field," he asked.

"Just a couple of weeks to be safe. I start PT tomorrow."

"Well, they'll miss you."

It was silent for sec as both of them reflected. Robin was the one to break the silence.

"Why do you always call me 'Big Sis'?"

"You're the biggest sister I have, and I don't ever want you to forget that."

Her tummy felt really warm inside as she started to blush a little.

"Get back on that field soon and be safe. Your team needs you as much as you need them."

Robin just smiled.

People started requesting Cal's presence in the other room.

"I'm going to go appease the masses—briefly," he said giving her a wink. "Don't go anywhere."

He headed out of the room.

"I won't."

She had her arms crossed, sitting in a daze. Robin released her arms and slid her right hand across the sofa. Alone in a room away from it all, she realized this is the best moment she's had—outside of sleeping. There were no questions, no looks of disapproval, no laughter that may-or-may-not-be *at* her; just Robin as her hand continued to slide along the sofa. Suddenly she felt someone—she flinched, looked up and noticed that no one was there.

Someone else's hand…?

I woke up and forgot that I was not at my house. I remember when it used to be my house. *It hasn't felt that way for a while.* Happens to everyone I guess. It was "up" time and I threw the blanket off of me. I was wearing my favorite lounge shirt. I'd had that t-shirt for like 10 years. When I first got it, it didn't even fit. Now it was a little tight on me. The fabric was warn from all of the washes, but you could still read the "Born to win losses" insignia on the front of it. I went up to my parent's dining room table and saw that they were in their PJs and bathrobes having their morning coffee. It was briefly awkward as I think I startled them.

"Matthew," my mom shrieked like she should be getting me something and forgot to. She got up and gave me a hug. I smiled and hugged her back.

"Hi son," said dad.

It really wasn't that awkward for my dad.

"Hi pop."

My mom walked over to the stove, "Do you want some coffee? I can make you some eggs."

"That would be great," I said.

I sat down across from my dad as he looked up at me and gave me a smile. He took a sip from his coffee. I gave a slight grin back. We never really talked that well in person. We got along, we just didn't talk. So when we found ourselves in situations like this, it was weird for both of us.

My mom brought over a cup of coffee and I thanked her. She made her way back to the stove and started humming an abstract tune.

I took a sip from my coffee.

My dad took a sip from his coffee.

...

I was about to say something-

"It's been warmer weather for this late in the year," he said.

"Yes it has," I replied.

We sat in another weird, long silence as my mom continued to cook and hum to herself. My dad would take another sip of his coffee, loud and hard in that silence. I would follow with a sip as well, not saying anything.

My mother finished the eggs and toast and I was able to break the silence with eating my food. Mom started to sniffle. I realized this had been the first time I'd seen my parents since they heard that Randy and I broke up. I started eating quicker, and I didn't look up from my plate. She pulled a wrinkled, dried up tissue from her robe pocket and blew her nose. I put my fork down.

"I'm so sorry Matthew."

"It's okay mom. I feel the same way."

"I just wish this never happened to you."

"Me too."

She blew her nose again and I pushed my plate away from me on the table. My dad started rubbing her shoulder and she held his hand. They looked at each other and smiled. I smiled because I didn't want to feel out of place. I look over at my dad and he lip-synced "Menopause." I held back a giggle. *That was needed.*

THANKSGIVING

I remember having a decent start to the morning. I got up around 8:30, magazine bathroom time, coffee at 9am, continued reading my magazine, sipping coffee at the table, set the mug down--

BOOM!

I was tackled out of my chair and hit the floor. Didn't see it coming.

"BUDDY BOY!"

My little brother, RJ happened. *Yay!* Young guy, stronger than he looks. I deserve every bit of physical punishment like that for the things I did to him growing up so there was no complaining at this point. Didn't mean it didn't hurt. Yes, I grimaced.

"Where's Randy," he asked.

Shit. Forgot to tell him.

He was still on top of me as I laid on my side. He appeared to be trying to get my left shoulder to meet my right shoulder face-to-face, unbeknownst to him I'm sure. I was running out of breath.

"Could you get off of me please," I said with shortness of breath.

"Sure bro."

Yes. He still calls people bro, not just me because I am his brother.

He helped me up.

"So, where's Randy?"

I dusted myself off and punched him square in the chin, knocking him to the floor. He got up holding his cheek.

"What the hell was that for?"

I don't know why I did it. It did feel good though. I don't think I was ready for a physical assault that morning, followed up with questions about my ex-girlfriend.

"For being an asshole," is all I said.

I grabbed my magazine and continued sipping my coffee at the table.

He yanked the magazine right out of my hands and glared at me.

"Where's Randy," he asked, slower and lower.

My mom came into the room and I looked at her.

"Mom, did you not tell him? He does live here you know."

"Tell him what," she asked, at the same time RJ asked, "Tell me what?"

I got up and left.

I saw my mom glare at him as I walked out.

"What did you do," she asked him as I left.

"Nothing," he replied. "I asked him where Randy was, that's all. Where the hell is she by the way, do you know?"

I could still overhear them arguing as I sat downstairs on the couch.

"I forgot to tell you. Randy left him a few weeks back."

"Well shit. I feel like an asshole. Why didn't anybody tell me?"

"I forgot. You know, you're always in and out of here so much we never know when you are here or for how long."

"Yeah, this is my fault...."

I got comfortable on the couch and dosed off to that noise.

* * *

I woke up to my family members laughing and conversing upstairs. I took a deep breath and headed up to meet the hoard. *In my "Born to win losses" T and pajama pants.* I get up there and all the noise stopped. Everyone was staring at me like I was an uncaged animal.

"Happy Thanksgiving everyone."

I started to tear up. *Shit you not.* Never made a larger

group of people feel that uncomfortable in my entire life. I rubbed my eyes dry, went over to the table and started filling up my plate.

My sweet mother leaned over and whispered to me, "We haven't blessed the food yet."

To which I replied, "Go ahead," while continuing to fill up my plate. "I'm a little mad at Him right now."

Judgment eyes from all around the room.

I just stood there with my arms crossed. My sister pulled everyone out of their misery and started reciting the Lord's Prayer. They all bowed their heads and echoed the procession.

"...hallowed be Thy name."

I grabbed a carrot and chomped it....loudly.

"...on Earth as it is in Heaven."

I grabbed some celery and did the same...only a little louder.

My sister and a few cousins started to giggle. That's all I wanted.

"...and forgive us our trespasses...."

Mom looked up and glared. *I kind of wanted that too— devil grin.*

"...but deliver us from evil...."

I grabbed a bottle of beer out of the cooler, popped the cap off onto the floor, took a swig, grabbed my plate, and went downstairs.

"...forever and ever. Amen."

After that weird silence, my dad said, "Well, let's eat."

I turned on the TV and started watching football. I was shortly joined by my uncles downstairs after they made their way through the buffet line. I was happy for the most part as they are not talkers. Then one of them asked me, "So, you got a girlfriend?"

I almost choked on my turkey. One good thing about

holidays like this is the amount of people under a small house. There were so many other conversations going on I did not get myself in trouble with a reply as my uncle had moved on to another conversation by the time I caught my breath. Now my other uncle who wears too much cologne and tries to dress younger than he can pull off asked me, "Do you go out dressed like that, because the sweats aren't doing it for me."

I was done eating so I went upstairs and dropped my plate off. I decided to have an Irish coffee so I sat down with some of my cousins. One of my aunts—pleasant lady, but has a conveyer belt moving without supply on the line—approached me.

"So where's Randy?"

Silence hit the room.

All she could do is look around at everybody, "What?"

I conversed with my cousins for a bit and decided that I wanted some pie. We all milled around and found some new seats. As I sat down to enjoy my slice, my other aunt had another lady next to her when she approached me. She was young compared to my aunt, but she was at least 15 years older than me.

"Matthew," said my aunt. "There is someone I'd like you to meet."

And here we go.

I rolled my eyes. I extended my hand to shake hers.

"I don't shake hands," she said. "Germs." *She was so proud.*

I just looked at her for a second...then...I couldn't contain it. I just started laughing. I almost choked on the last bite of pie that I had taken. My poor aunt just stood there with a concerned smile while the lady stared at me. I got up and excused myself from the room, just laughing my fat, pie-eating face off.

I can only describe the next few hours as question hell.

Quirky-out-of-the-woodwork relative after relative asking me questions I never wanted to hear/answer...*EVER*.

"Do you think you two will get back together...?"

"What are you going to do when you graduate...?"

"You're not gay, are you...?"

"Is your hair starting to gray...?"

"Why don't you ever come and see us...?"

"Call me, we'll talk..."

"Call me. Any time..."

CALL ME! CALL ME! CALL ME!

Ugh. It was the worst kind of peer pressure. You would end up doing something you know you shouldn't, and you wouldn't even get high. No thank you.

When everybody left and I had a moment by myself on the love seat, I felt a weird sense of relief and exhaustion. I took my glasses off and rubbed my temples. I dropped my left hand down to the sofa and I couldn't believe what I felt. Now I know it sounds crazy, but I swear I felt someone's hand. I flinched my hand back and looked around the room. The second after I did that, I wished I hadn't. There was something about it that was comforting, however brief it was.

Robin laid in bed in her pajamas in total silence. It was dead week on campus and most of the milling and jostling that occurred in the dorm was non-existent as everyone was sleeping in from all-nighters or already at their morning classes. Robin still wore her neck brace to bed as she rolled onto her back and stared at the ceiling. She heard a knock on a door down the hall and didn't think much of it. The door was answered and there was muffled dialogue. There was a sudden knock on her door as well as she was slightly startled and annoyed that she had to get up. She looked through the peephole and there was a man wearing an Afro wig and sunglasses dressed in a bathrobe carrying flyers. He waved. She opened the door as the man opened his robe. Robin, shocked at first, saw a poster board covering his body that had holiday party info on it. There was noise down the hall and the man at her door looked in that direction.

"Oh shit," he said. "Here, disperse the rest of these please?"

He handed Robin the flyers as the majority of them scattered to the floor. He raced down the hall. Two campus security guards zoomed past her door. She closed her door and ran to her window. Outside, on the Quad, she noticed the same guy racing across the grounds as the two guards were gaining on him. Bored, Robin grabbed a flyer and read the announcement. It was the same information that was on the body billboard. Robin decided to help out and took the remainder of the flyers down the hall, sliding one under each door.

Robin went back to her room to study.

Missy burst through her door.

"You will not believe what just happened."

Robin, unenthused and in no mood for Missy right now

stated, "I think it won't be that amazing."

Missy, ignoring her, goes right into her story, "I was walking back from a study group and this tall guy runs past me. I didn't think much of it at first, but he came back and stopped in front of me and said hello. I was a little startled at first, but he was smiling. He had a great smile. Then, he said how are you and BOOM-"

Robin wasn't ready for that.

"...he gets gang tackled by two security guards. It happened so fast, I didn't know what to think. They cuffed him and drug him off, each holding an arm. He had a bloody lip from the tackle and he didn't stop looking into my eyes as they took him away..."

Robin nonchalantly replied, "He stopped by up here. He gave me these flyers to pass out."

Robin handed Missy a flyer.

"I put them under everyone's door."

"Robin," said Missy. "He's friends with that guy you like. I'll bet he'll be there, we have to go."

"I know he'll be there," she replied. "He's the host."

Missy is confused, "How do you know?"

"I've been there, remember?"

...

"You slut," replied Missy.

"You know it wasn't like that."

"Look Rob, this party is going to be fun. We're going."

Robin turned and looked right through Missy, "I know."

Missy was dumbfounded when Robin smiled at her. Missy started to smile back as they both giggled. Missy ran to Robin and gave her a big hug.

LATER

Robin (without her neck brace) and Missy approached

Matthew's front door. Robin took a deep breath and raised her hand to knock, but Missy stepped in and held her arm back.

"This is your night Robin."

Robin stared at her, confused.

"Don't look at me like I'm crazy," continued Missy. "You're going to meet someone tonight. He may not be your dream guy. He may not be the man you will marry, he most likely won't even be someone you'll want to date, but you are going to meet someone and have fun tonight."

"You make me sound desperate....and lonely."

"That's not what I mean," she replied.

Missy took a moment to collect her thoughts and continued, "You are going to meet a guy—cute or not—and give him your phone number. He will call you in a couple days and you will go out with him on a date and decide if you like him. You'll judge him on his appearance and manners. You'll notice if he smells nice right away and if he does, you'll believe that it's a good start with your date and move along with the anticipation of what's to come. If he takes you to a nice place to eat, that is an okay date, but, if he takes you bowling, to an arcade, for a walk on the greenbelt, to play ski ball, whatever; you'll find him inventive, loosen up, and feel that he is interested...like you. You'll get to know each other better and learn the simple things; colors, movies, television, and if you're lucky, you'll agree on some of those things. When the night is over, yet still young, he'll take you home, walk you to the front door, and want to kiss you goodnight. I think you should let him. If you do, you'll have more dates and he will get anxious about your first time."

"I've had sex," Robin interjected.

"Not with him. Trust me, he'll be anxious. If you like him and you think he can handle it, you'll make him wait. But, if you *really* like him, you won't want to wait...but you will because you know he might be the right kind of person to earn it."

Robin rolled her eyes.

"Don't do that. I think I'm psyching you out now. That's not what I'm trying to do-"

"What are you doing exactly?"

"I don't know…I just want you to meet someone worth dating. We're in college and I'd hate to see you miss out on meeting a guy or two before you graduate."

"I've met guys."

"I meant guys that aren't named *Max*. How'd you meet him, anyway?"

"He was my lab partner in Biology," said Robin. "What are we doing? Can we go inside now?"

"Yes, in a minute, I just…I just can't wait for you that's all. In a good way. I mean, it's hard for me to say…I have had some relationships and the beginning is always the best part when you meet someone that you enjoy being around…the inside of your tummy starts to get warm when you think about them when they're not around and you tend to smile like an idiot without even knowing it—and you don't care, because you can't wait to see them again…"

Robin squinted at her with a raised eyebrow.

"I want you to find *the beginning* with someone. That's the best part. You're my best friend and you deserve it and I want you to have it…"

Robin started to feel bad, a little and decided to give the appearance that she was listening.

"There's a lot of good that comes with *the beginning* besides the butterflies, the giggles, losing your train of thought thinking about them in math lab...that's when you know the sex will be great."

Robin blushed. No one could tell outside with just the porch light on, but she felt the skin on her face warm up.

Missy just continued, in a daze and didn't notice.

"That first time is always such a bumble of wonderful. You start with a kiss, then the kiss becomes deeper, longer and the blood in your veins starts to run hot. You both lose a little bit of control with your hands and forget they're there. The blunder comes when you start to move into position and attempt to undo each other's clothes. It's new to both of you so you want to keep your eyes closed and continue kissing--buttons and latches always complicate things. You both give up briefly on all of the undoing and just grind your hips against each other's middle when you feel it rub against you for the first time and now you *have to* figure out how to undo his pants as both of your sighs get a little louder. You have to pull away and look down at his waist, quickly enough to undo the clasp and pull the zipper down. He uses this moment to do the same and then you're both back at kissing as you put your hand down his pants and his down yours."

"Missy-"

"That's all. I'm excited for you right now and I hope that tonight turns out fun for you…and honestly, I hope that this isn't the last night in college that you find *the beginning* with someone."

Robin pondered then grinned at Missy, "I hear you. I promise I'll be fun tonight."

"That's all I ask. Give 'em a chance," commanded Missy with a wink as she opened the door and entered the house.

The pollution of loud music hit the air as Robin followed her in.

Missy and Robin flowed into a room swamped with mingling bodies. People were smoking and drinking as they all bumped into each other, making their way to the keg in the kitchen.   Missy and Robin rubbed shoulder-to-shoulder with everyone as they slowly squeezed toward the kitchen them-selves.

Robin lost Missy in the crowd and tried to find her. She bumped her back into someone who turned to see her when she apologized.

IT WAS MAX!

He looked shocked and embarrassed.

Robin was uncomfortable and felt she should say some-thing, but couldn't...

Max tried to avoid eye contact while remaining speech-less.

Robin continued to look at him, not knowing where she could run. She really wished she had Missy as a buffer.

Max finally looked away and continued his conversa-tion with his friends, giving them both great relief.

Feeling like she dodged a major bullet, Robin continued to search for Missy. After squeezing through another barrage of backsides, arms, elbows and shoulders, she finally found Missy —making out in the kitchen next to the keg with the "flyer boy."

She felt happy for her friend but noticed that she was probably watching the two of them make out a little longer than she should have…so she went outside on the porch.

It was really weird. Davy, Brock, and Billy were all at my house studying. It was quite peaceful and I was feeling quite productive.

"Well," said Brock, standing up.

There went that.

"It's that time of year again," he finished.

We all looked at him, confused. In fairness, our brains were mush from all of the reading/studying/quizzing.

"Straws or delegating for flyer patrol?"

I was utterly confused now.

Does he know he's hurting, not helping?

"What," I asked.

He opened up my coat closet and pulled out a suit bag. I immediately went back to studying as I knew what he was talking about now and had no desire to go there. Billy and Davy were still confused so he continued to unzip the suit bag as an Afro wig, a robe, and glasses-with-a-nose popped out. Billy and Davy looked uncomfortable when they saw it now.

"I was on flyer duty last year bitches, so I'm not going," he continued.

I asked, "Where's the party this year," knowing full well those assholes planned to use my place as they had nowhere else to go.

"Well, I thought we'd have it here like we always do," said Brock.

I kept looking into my book.

"I don't feel like hosting a party this year."

"Well where else are we going to have it?"

I really wanted to hurt him and my face showed it. Brock took a step back when I looked at him. I looked at the other assholes and they were pleading with him.

"I'm not on flyer patrol."

"I will wash your car," said Billy to Brock.

Davy threw Billy a look like the one I had just thrown Brock.

Davy grabbed the gear and left.

We didn't hear from him until the party a few days later. Apparently he got in trouble and had to do a few hours of campus service for hanging out in the girls dorms during dead week. Anyway, party on.

* * *

So here we are. Loud music, Mary Jane, beer, boys, ladies and friends with girlfriends. Some of them anyway. Billy is standing outside the bathroom door waiting for Ashley to come out victorious.

"Ash," he asks, gently knocking on the door. "You okay? Ash?"

No answer. He notices me noticing him.

"Hey Matt. Great party."

"Everything okay," I ask him, knowing fully well that it's not.

"Yeah man, she just had a little too much to drink."

Ashley opens the door and walks out in front of Billy. She is using all the strength she has to gag back what's left in her stomach. *Brother, I do not miss that.* She heads back into the bathroom again and this time, Billy follows her in there.

I notice Davy leaned up against the wall people watching and decide to say, "Hi."

I lean up against the wall next to him and he gets up off the wall and starts talking to that girl he met at the bar last week. I smile and decide to go get a beer. On my way over, I notice Brock and Kathy actually having a civil interaction. She giggles and gives him a kiss. *Weird.* I finish my beer and start filling another. If you recall, I was enjoying my beer next to the keg for a moment when I noticed a woman walk out onto the porch. Are you back with me now?

Fuck it! I'm gonna go talk to her. I felt confident… then I spilled my beer on me when a couple next to me decided to get "make-out unaware." Now I'm a little angry and anxious.

Sound familiar yet?

When I realized it was Davy and "the bar girl," I stopped being upset and that gave me courage again for some odd reason.

"*I'm so happy…I'm so lonely…Sunday morning is every day…Light my candles in a daze….YEAHHHHH,*" blares the music.

Yes, she is still over there on the porch, and yes, I'm going to go talk to her right now.

As I approach her, I feel my heart beating faster and everything feels like it's in slow motion. It gets to the point that all I hear is my heartbeat and I'm having second thoughts…but I just kept walking.

I just say the first thing that pops into my head, "I can change the music if that will help."

I think I startled her a little, but she's being nice about it.

She looks back at me but it's pretty dark outside since my porch light is out at the moment.

She didn't get a very good look at me….this could work!

"No," she says. "It's not the music, I just needed some air…it was a rough semester."

I make my way across the porch and lean on the railing next to her.

"I hear you. Don't get me started."

"I'm a little frustrated," she continues. "I came here to have fun and relax but I don't think that I know how. I've been here five minutes and I wish I was back in my dorm, studying. My best friend in there—Missy—she has been here five minutes and has already gotten comfortable. Come on! I don't necessarily envy that attribute all the time, but on nights like tonight I wish I was a little like her...a little."

I check the rest of my beer and offer it to her. She takes it and continues. That was the coolest thing that happened to me in a long time. I didn't think she'd actually take my beer.

"I mean, she can talk to anyone, anywhere," she takes a sip. "This is really good," as she takes another sip. "She is *so* confident. I can't talk to anybody, generally," taking another drink.

"You're doing all right."

"I'm sorry I'm carrying on. I must sound so pathetic..."

Instantly I think of my most pathetic moment standing alone at the theater ticket line: "*One for 'Clueless' please.*"

I turn and look at her, "You're not pathetic."

"Thank you."

"Besides, it's easy for girls to be confident. You have the advantage."

"How's that?"

"Well, ultimately it is up to you on how our evening will end up so there are factors there that allow you to dictate the future. It should be real easy for all girls to talk to any guy. We need guidance. That's why we're called guys."

"Any guy? Come on, you don't seriously believe that. I can't just walk up to Johnny Depp and start up a conversation."

"You better be able to. How often are you going to see Johnny Depp in your lifetime? Besides, he's seeing a hot French woman. It wouldn't work out any way, but it never hurts to ask. They may have an open relationship... she is French."

Three way!

She giggles and takes another drink.

"It's just different for guys," I continue. "There is that pressure that we have to be the ones to go to you. I mean, wasn't women's lib supposed to take care of that?"

"No, women's lib made it okay for women to pick up other women."

I let out a large laugh...the embarrassing kind. She was drinking at the time and laughed at my laugh, causing beer to go out her mouth and nose. *Classy.*

"That is a great laugh," she replies.

"Okay, okay. I know, it is annoying and loud, but that was really unexpected and funny."

"No, no. I *really* like your laugh. It's cute."

Thankfully it was too dark for her to see me blush. There was uncomfortable silence. She was kind enough to clear her throat and take another sip.

"I am sorry. I really don't know what to say right now."

She giggles, "You don't have to say anything, just enjoy this quiet, klutzy moment."

"Not helping. I need conversation. It makes me feel like I'm doing something right."

We look at each other. It's too dark to really see each other.

"You're doing fine," she says, putting her free hand on my wrist. "You have a wonderful laugh."

"I have to admit. I shocked myself with that laugh. It has been a while since I laughed that hard. Like you said, rough semester."

"Well, I needed a laugh. Sorry for laughing at *your* expense."

"It's okay, my *"friends"* have prepared me for such a moment. They laugh at my stupid ass all the time."

She laughs now.

I'm going to keep going.

"It's not entirely their fault. I tend to do and say some

pretty stupid shit."

She lets out a giggle as we turn and look at each other again. I feel like the cloud cover moved, exposing us to the moonlight then-

"ROBIN!"

"MATTHEW!"

She knows who I am?

This was the first time my life "flashed before my eyes." I remembered seeing her in the stands right before I got pummeled in the head with the ball, I remembered watching her score a goal, I remembered seeing her soccer photo online, I remembered seeing her get kissed by that jackass outside her dorm—*I hate that guy*—I remembered seeing her get injured at her game, and I remembered hearing her say, "I *really* like your laugh. It's cute."

"Would you like to go and get a cup of coffee with me some time?"

It just flew out of my mouth.

She looks away and has to think about it as she probably wasn't ready for the question.

Not going to lie. Little concerned at this point.

I sit and wait as she turns and meets my eyes with hers. I think she's grinning, slightly.

Hope she says yes.

Thank you…

….for using your precious time to read this very personal story that I felt compelled to tell. My hope is that you enjoyed it as much as I enjoyed writing it. Okay, maybe a little better than that (writing is arduous). There are plenty more to come and your support will help them come even faster. If you have a few moments more, please add a quick, honest review on Amazon or any other format you're comfortable with.

SNEAK PEEK

Yes. Another one. I've started it at least. No promises on the release date yet. I'll keep you posted on my newsletter, blog, twitter.com at @clintingtons, etc. It is currently *untitled*.

(1)

She remembered the rain.

There were a lot of performances over the years, but that night, she made note of the rain in the back alley entrance to the stage. The drops were rather large, and they were coming down pretty hard and fast.

She sat in a daze on her couch that morning, holding her coffee in her hand, recalling the night before.

Generally, before a performance, she was numb. Not this time. She was nervous, almost sick and her hands trembled.

She took a sip of her coffee while in a trance and remembered the start of it.

Darkness.

Always darkness to start.

It was when the blast of the electronic dance music kicked in that the lights came up and Sam announced her presence on the stage with her standard front-flip-to-her-feet off of a 6 foot platform in the dark, with her violin in hand. She ripped off the harness with her bow hand immediately after landing. The harness—that the building managers always insisted she wear—just got in the way. She hated it. She didn't need it.

As the tempo of the dubstep continued, Sam unleashed music from her violin and the stadium roared with approval. Her company of stage dancers had appeared from the background as Sam continued to make beautiful tones scream from her kit, in tune with the rhythm of the dubstep. The dancers formed their line along her right and left and started matching her synchronization of the movement of Sam's legs and feet.

The stadium began to clap in unison with the beat as Sam and her troupe continued their routine. The dancers made their way behind Sam in a line and she paused her play as she took a back flip back, and the dancers spread away on the floor like battered bowling pins in graceful unison. Sam then sprung a flip forward again and went into her violin solo as the dancers gathered equally to her right and left, continuing their unison dance movements.

Sam remembered losing herself into the violin in that moment and did not want to wake from the dream. The searing melody was epic as the beat stopped and the baseline accompanied her.

She was no longer in a roaring stadium. The violin and bow were an extension of her self as they communicated with each other. She wished that this could be the rest of her life, but this song was coming to a close.

Only one song. It doesn't seem right.

The drums kicked back in as she finished her solo and continued the rhythmic flow of the song from her instrument.

Drawing to a close on this opening number, she remembered the light and smoke show going off at the conclusion and cutting to total darkness again as she dropped below the stage.

In a flash the lights were up again and the violin was playing with the electronic dance music. Sam walked under stage right, hit the stairs and looked back at herself playing on the stage before leaving for the evening. It was her sound, but it was a phantom of her and she wanted the authenticity of the evening to extend longer than it did, but that had passed. She was on to other things.

Slipping out the empty alley, she pulled her black cloak over head to protect her from the rain until she reached her motorcycle. She took down her hood, strapped on her black helmet, dug her feet in deep, and skidded out of the alley into the night. She drove for miles outside of the city limits until she reached the bottom of a hill and looked up at the house she was making a visit to.

This is where the memory became choppy for Sam, taking another sip of her coffee. Her eyes were open, but she was only seeing the frames in her head.

She remembered debugging the alarms, a mild buzz as the back door swung open for her entrance. Her footsteps could not be heard on the floor. Slowly, she went up the steps and around a hall into the master bedroom. She remembered pulling something from her cloak as she approached the bed, an older, balding man with a gray beard lace face up in deep rest as she continued toward him. Without hesitation, she quickly jammed the object into the man's chest and covered his mouth as his scream was muffled. She could feel her hand get wet with his breath and saliva. His body tensed and he wanted to move, but he was paralyzed as smoke started to escape his mouth, nose, and eyes. thirty seconds more and the man stopped struggling. Another 15 seconds and his eyes rolled back into his head.

She closed his eyelids like a priest might, and left.

She sipped her coffee in a daze again as her doorbell rang, zapping her vision into reality.

She got up and shut her robe around her body with her belt and answered the door.

"What the hell do *you* want?"

For all the current happenings…

…you can join my email list:

http://eepurl.com/bhD6qb

I generally put out one a month and talk about movies, television, and the status of my writing in general.

About the author...

...Clintington was born and raised in and around Idaho and has lived there the majority of his life. He has been a cook, a dispatcher, a camera man, a video editor, a sandwich maker, a donut fryer, a direct care staff, a developmental specialist, a policy writer, and a social media content editor. If he's not at work, watching football, or writing—he's most likely with his son, at a park or on the beautiful greenbelt. He managed to earn a degree in television broadcast, and like most people, doesn't currently use his degree in his field...He lives in southwest Idaho with his son.

Website: clintington.com
Amazon Author Page: https://authorcentral.amazon.com/gp/profile
Twitter: @clintingtons
Facebook: https://www.facebook.com/clint.harrington.526

www.ingramcontent.com/pod-product-compliance
Lightning Source LLC
Chambersburg PA
CBHW060434130626
46555CB00005B/2346